MW00874101

Prophecy

The Queen's Alpha Series, Volume 7

W.J. May

Published by Dark Shadow Publishing, 2018.

This is a work of fiction. Similarities to real people, places, or events are entirely coincidental.

PROPHECY

First edition. September 15, 2018.

Copyright © 2018 W.J. May.

Written by W.J. May.

Also by W.J. May

Bit-Lit Series
Lost Vampire
Cost of Blood
Price of Death

Blood Red Series
Courage Runs Red
The Night Watch
Marked by Courage
Forever Night

Daughters of Darkness: Victoria's Journey
Victoria
Huntress
Coveted (A Vampire & Paranormal Romance)
Twisted
Daughter of Darkness - Victoria - Box Set

Hidden Secrets Saga
Seventh Mark - Part 1
Seventh Mark - Part 2
Marked By Destiny
Compelled
Fate's Intervention
Chosen Three
The Hidden Secrets Saga: The Complete Series

Kerrigan Chronicles
Stopping Time
A Passage of Time
Ticking Clock

Mending Magic Series
Lost Souls
Illusion of Power

Paranormal Huntress Series
Never Look Back
Coven Master
Alpha's Permission
Blood Bonding
Oracle of Nightmares
Shadows in the Night
Paranormal Huntress BOX SET #1-3

Prophecy Series
Only the Beginning
White Winter
Secrets of Destiny

The Chronicles of Kerrigan
Rae of Hope
Dark Nebula
House of Cards
Royal Tea
Under Fire
End in Sight
Hidden Darkness
Twisted Together
Mark of Fate
Strength & Power
Last One Standing
Rae of Light
The Chronicles of Kerrigan Box Set Books # 1 - 6

The Chronicles of Kerrigan: Gabriel
Living in the Past
Present For Today
Staring at the Future

The Chronicles of Kerrigan Prequel

Christmas Before the Magic
Question the Darkness
Into the Darkness
Fight the Darkness
Alone in the Darkness
Lost in Darkness
The Chronicles of Kerrigan Prequel Series Books #1-3

The Chronicles of Kerrigan Sequel
A Matter of Time
Time Piece
Second Chance
Glitch in Time
Our Time
Precious Time

The Hidden Secrets Saga
Seventh Mark (part 1 & 2)

The Queen's Alpha Series
Eternal
Everlasting
Unceasing
Evermore
Forever
Boundless
Prophecy
Protected

Foretelling

The Senseless Series
Radium Halos
Radium Halos - Part 2
Nonsense

Standalone
Shadow of Doubt (Part 1 & 2)
Five Shades of Fantasy
Shadow of Doubt - Part 1
Shadow of Doubt - Part 2
Four and a Half Shades of Fantasy
Dream Fighter
What Creeps in the Night
Forest of the Forbidden
Arcane Forest: A Fantasy Anthology
The First Fantasy Box Set

Watch for more at https://www.facebook.com/USA-TODAY-Best-seller-WJ-May-Author-141170442608149/.

THE QUEEN'S ALPHA SERIES

PROPHECY

USA TODAY BESTSELLING AUTHOR
W.J. MAY

Copyright 2018 by W.J. May

THE QUEEN'S ALPHA SERIES
PROPHECY
USA TODAY BESTSELLING AUTHOR
W.J. MAY

THIS E-BOOK IS LICENSED for your personal enjoyment only. This e-book may not be re-sold or given away to other people. If you would like to share this book with another person, please purchase an additional copy for each recipient. If you're reading this book and did not purchase it, or it was not purchased for your use only, then please return to Smashwords.com and purchase your own copy. Thank you for respecting the hard work of the author.

All rights reserved. No part of this publication may be reproduced, stored in or introduced into a retrieval system, or transmitted, in any form, or by any means (electronic, mechanical, photocopying, recording, or otherwise) without the prior written permission of both the copyright owner and the above publisher of this book.

This is a work of fiction. Names, characters, places, brands, media, and incidents are either the product of the author's imagination or are used fictitiously. Any resemblance to actual person, living or dead, events, or locales is entirely coincidental. The author acknowledges the trademarked status and trademark owners of various products referenced in this work of fiction, which have been used without permission. The publication/use of these trademarks is not authorized, associated with, or sponsored by the trademark owners.

All rights reserved.

Copyright 2018 by W.J. May1

Prophecy, Book 7 of the Queen's Alpha Series

Cover design by: Book Cover by Design

No part of this book may be used or reproduced in any manner whatsoever without written permission, except in the case of brief quotations embodied in articles and reviews.

THE QUEEN'S ALPHA SERIES

PROPHECY

USA TODAY BESTSELLING AUTHOR

W. J. MAY

Have You Read the C.o.K Series?

The Chronicles of Kerrigan
Book I - *Rae of Hope* is FREE!

BOOK TRAILER:

http://www.youtube.com/watch?v=gILAwXxx8MU

How hard do you have to shake the family tree to find the truth about the past?

Fifteen year-old Rae Kerrigan never really knew her family's history. Her mother and father died when she was young and it is only when she accepts a scholarship to the prestigious Guilder Boarding School in England that a mysterious family secret is revealed.

Will the sins of the father be the sins of the daughter?

As Rae struggles with new friends, a new school and a star-struck forbidden love, she must also face the ultimate challenge: receive a tattoo on her sixteenth birthday with specific powers that may bind her to an unspeakable darkness. It's up to Rae to undo the dark evil in her family's past and have a ray of hope for her future.

Find W.J. May

Website:
http://www.wanitamay.yolasite.com
Facebook:
https://www.facebook.com/pages/Author-WJ-May-FAN-PAGE/
141170442608149
Newsletter:
SIGN UP FOR W.J. May's Newsletter to find out about new releases,
updates, cover reveals and even freebies!
http://eepurl.com/97aYf

Prophecy Blurb:

S he will fight for what is hers.

The five kingdoms may have been saved, but the battle is far from won.

Katerina Damaris finally takes her place on the throne, only to realize that the crown isn't what she thought it would be. Friends become kingdoms. Lovers become a liability. Secret promises are broken to protect the greater good.

Caught in the middle of political circus, Katerina must choose between ruling her kingdom or following her heart. Alliances are strained, borders are tested, and whispers of an old enemy resurrected hang like a shadow over the realm.

Can Katerina keep the peace? Will the five kingdoms ever be truly reunited?

Most importantly, can she and the others figure out the prophecy in time?

Be careful who you trust. Even the devil was once an angel.

The Queen's Alpha Series

Eternal
Everlasting
Unceasing
Evermore
Forever
Boundless
Prophecy
Protected
Foretelling
Revelation
Betrayal
Resolved

Chapter 1

S he took him by surprise.

That alone was almost impossible to do. She'd tried it in every kingdom, at every hour, in every situation you could possibly think of. It had only happened twice.

Third time's the charm...

He was standing on the balcony when she slipped inside the room. His eyes fixed on the horizon. His head a million miles away. Both arms were hanging by his sides, deceptively still, but the fingers on one hand kept twitching, like he was playing out a rhythm no one else could hear.

The world outside was in a happy sort of chaos.

The villagers had been lighting bonfires for days, getting ready for the big celebration. More and more people poured in every hour, and the sky at dusk was filled with sparks and smoke. They swirled in slow-moving columns towards the sky, a lazy dance of shadow and light.

She was careful. Stepping only on her toes. Holding her breath whenever possible. She had learned long ago not to startle this particular group of friends, and Dylan was harder than most. The man didn't take kindly to surprises, as he tended to react with a blade.

So, it was with the utmost caution and the utmost pride that she ghosted across the room and joined him on the stone ledge. Thrilled with her success. Amazed he didn't hear her.

It's the carpet, she thought. *That's why he hates the carpet.*

Her body coiled like a kitten waiting to pounce. A look of wicked triumph flashed through her eyes. Then, with a burst of unnatural speed, she threw herself into the air.

Success!

Her hands clapped over his eyes and he let out a startled gasp. The body froze. The fingers stopped twitching. Of course, such things only ever lasted for a moment. Before the princess could begin to revel in her victory, he whirled around in a fluid movement. Knocking her off balance and catching her in the inescapable circle of his arms.

"What have I told you about doing that?"

His voice was stern, but his eyes were all sparkles. For a moment, she was reminded of the ranger she met in the tavern all those months ago. Playfully taunting a group of vampires. Deadly talents, with a secret smile tugging at the edges of his lips.

"I'm sorry." Her voice trembled as she stared up at him with a pair of enormous, fearful eyes, fighting back a smile of her own. "Sometimes I forget."

An eyebrow rose ever so slightly. A shiver ran down her spine.

"Is that right?" He released her with a chilling smile, bowing his head so they were at the same level. "Well, I'm afraid *sorry* isn't good enough."

Their eyes met and she sucked in a silent breath.

"I'll just have to teach you to remember..."

For a moment, the world stood still. Then it was Dylan's turn to pounce.

"Guards!" Katerina let out a wild shriek, streaking towards the door, knowing for a fact that she would never make it.

Sure enough, he caught her a second later. Laughing loudly as he spun her around. "Don't *actually* call for your guards, crazy!" He hoisted her into the air, sweeping back her hair with a breathless smile. "We're in your castle, not mine! They'll run me through!"

"Good." She wrapped her legs around his waist, flushed and grinning. "Someone has to teach you some manners."

These games of theirs had gotten increasingly intense. Ever since that shadowy dragon fell out of the sky and they'd decided never to leave each other's chambers.

"Manners, huh?" His eyes raked over her with a shameless smile, lingering on all his favorite parts. "I was under the impression you liked me rather... unmannered."

A flaming blush heated her cheeks, but she refused to give an inch. Quite the contrary, she unwrapped her legs and slid gracefully to the ground. Acting as though she hadn't heard. "In your dreams, peasant. Now get yourself together. It's time for the banquet."

The game came to a sudden end as the smile melted slowly off his face.

"The banquet?" There was a visible slump to his shoulders and his eyes flickered towards the door, like at any moment the hordes of people might come storming inside. "That's tonight?"

Katerina stopped searching for his shoes long enough to give him an exasperated smile. "The whole palace has been talking about it for weeks." She gestured towards the balcony where they had both just been standing. "You were literally just watching them put up the tents."

"...and here I thought the circus was in town."

"Have you been to a royal banquet?" she snorted sarcastically, digging around in his piles of discarded weaponry for a second shoe. "You're not too far off—"

She let out a gasp as he lifted her into the air. Cradling her in his arms. Staring down with a dimpled smile. A smile she knew very well. A smile he used when he wanted something.

"I have a better idea."

She shook her head with a wry grin. "Oh, this I have to hear."

"...let's *not* go to the banquet."

"Shocker."

"Let's stay here and get naked instead."

Already, he had somehow managed to slip out of his shirt. The pants were soon to follow. A shiver of anticipation shot down Katerina's spine, but she was quick to reject it. And avert her eyes.

"You are, without a doubt, the *worst* royal in the history of royalty." She shimmied out of his hands, landing with a soft thud upon the floor. "I don't want to go any more than you do, but we have to be there. How would it look if the king of Belaria and queen of the High Kingdom—"

"I feel like you're not taking my idea very seriously." He scooped her off her feet once again, tossing her carelessly over his shoulder. "Allow me to convince you."

"Wait! Dylan—no!" She giggled and shrieked, pounding uselessly on his back as she was carried towards the bed. "We can't, I'm serious! The delegations are already sitting down! I just came up here to get you—"

"—and now you have me."

He dropped her in the center of the mattress and waited. Enchanting eyes. Sculpted muscles. Messy hair. Wearing nothing but a toe-curling smile. Just waiting for her to decide.

Oh, come on, how is that fair?!

"What's it going to be, princess?" he prompted with a devilish smile, tugging her dress just hard enough that it slipped off her shoulders. "The banquet, or..."

She didn't answer. She grabbed him instead.

The next second, they were crashing together. Lips crushing lips. Arms and legs tangling in the sheets. His fingers scrambling against the back of her dress.

A breathless display of lust and passion, tempered only when he pulled back with a frown and actually peeked over her shoulder at the complicated corset he was attempting to untie.

"Hang on... I think it's locked or something."

She pushed up on her elbows with an exasperated grin, trying and failing to knock aside his hands. "It's not locked, just let me do it."

"...where did I put my knife?"

"No—absolutely not!" She scrambled back to the headboard, lifting a threatening finger in the air between them. "I'm serious, you *can-*

not just keep cutting them off like that! What am I supposed to say to the seamstress?"

"That you hope she finds a man as resourceful as me?"

"Dylan!"

"Doesn't matter, leave it on." He hitched up the skirt with a heated grin, running his hands up the length of her thighs. "I prefer a bit of a challenge—"

A loud knock froze them both in place. Another knock and they sprang apart.

"Just how many people were you expecting tonight?" Dylan muttered, shooting his girlfriend a hard look as she lobbed a pair of pants into his face.

"Would you just *get dressed*," she hissed, trying desperately to smooth down her tangled mess of hair. "It's bad enough the maids find you in here almost every morning—"

"Milady?" an apologetic voice filtered through the door.

Dylan dropped back onto the bed, pressing a pillow over his face. "Tell them to go away."

"Yes?" Katerina called, ignoring the man sulking in front of her. "What is it?"

"Milady, you told us to wake you when the first of the envoys arrived."

...wake me?

She and Dylan shared a strange glance.

Why would they need to wake me? I'm already—

"MILADY?"

Katerina shot up with a gasp. One hand clutching her chest. The other clutching the empty mattress beside her. The Dylan of her dreams was gone. Her pesky corset was propped up on the chair. And the dusky twilight was replaced with the crisp air of early morning.

"Your Majesty?" the voice called again.

"I'm up!" The sound of scurrying footsteps faded quickly down the hall, and Katerina dropped back to the mattress with a groan. "I'm up."

Her dreams had been rather vivid ever since returning to the castle. Vivid, and the damn things always seemed to stop at exactly the wrong moment. She squeezed her eyes shut with equal parts amusement and frustration. The sheets around her felt empty and cold.

Doesn't take a genius to interpret that one.

With a quiet sigh she pushed to her feet and padded across the thick carpet, throwing open the curtains to let in the magnificent sunrise. For a moment, she simply stared. Freezing like a statue in the window, while the morning rays danced in her hair and glinted off the pendant on her neck.

The grounds were abuzz with activity—very much the way it was in her dream.

People were pitching tents. Setting up chairs. Hauling in barrels upon barrels of food. The royal chefs hadn't slept a wink in the last forty-eight hours, and already the smells of a grand feast were wafting up through the castle halls. Groundskeepers had been brought in from every corner of the five kingdoms to masterfully sculpt the garden and lawns. Fire-dancers and a Tengali choir had been booked for entertainment. Nine separate crystal foundations had been commissioned for the occasion, and the royal florist had been working morning to night.

And that was all for the *outside*. For the commoners. The *inside* of the castle was even worse.

Katerina swore she had never seen such dedication. Such a fierce need to prove oneself and impress all at the same time. The servants and staff had banded together like an army, throwing their bodies into the fray and vowing to leave no man behind.

The tapestries had been taken down and dusted. Every stone from the dungeon to the top of the northern tower had been scrubbed to a shine. The blood had been discreetly removed from the corridors, and on every flat surface were bouquets of flowers in vases of pearl.

Normally, all these things would have made Katerina happy. Normally, she'd be racing down the stairs, delighting in the smell of fresh peonies, pestering the chef for a taste of things to come.

As it was, she simply closed the curtains with a tired sigh.

That morning somehow felt different than all the rest. As of that morning, she had officially been back at the castle for longer than she had been away.

It wasn't a terrible thing, of course. It had been her goal the whole time. To return to the halls of her childhood home. To take up the crown and claim what was rightfully hers. Her welcome back had been more than she could have imagined—once she fought past the army trying to stop it and cleaned off the blood. Those nobles who had been silenced in her absence returned jubilantly to court. The remnants of the old regime were promptly destroyed, and the new Damaris dynasty was ushered in with exaltation and festivity the likes of which the realm had never seen.

Yes, it was everything she'd ever wanted. The dream for which she'd almost given her life.

But she couldn't help feeling as though she'd left a part of herself on the road, roaming the five kingdoms with her friends. That her travels had claimed a piece of her she might never get back.

"Milady?" That faceless voice again. The one that plagued her even in dreams. "Would you like me to help you get ready? I can send for a bottle of Champagne—"

"No, thank you. I can get ready myself."

Bold words. Ones that would have shocked her old governess and earned her a well-deserved slap across the face. Royalty did not 'do it themselves.' That's what servants were for.

But things had changed. *She* had changed. And no one dared question the queen.

After cracking a window to let in the brisk morning air, she hurried to her closet before the servants could return for round two. Pushing aside the fancier, embroidered numbers, she reached all the way to the back and found what she was looking for. A simple dress of sky blue silk. Not unlike the one a certain ranger had stolen for her several weeks before.

She slipped it over her head with a wistful smile, suddenly feeling as though she'd give anything for whiskey and biscuits out in the woods.

For once, the newly-crowned Katerina Damaris was not the primary focus as she made her way down the halls. In fact, people were rushing by so quickly most of them hardly spared her a second glance. It was day one of the Accords. A massive peace summit that she and the rest of her friends had spent the last few months painstakingly engineering. Never before had so many different people gathered under one roof, and the castle was in a collective panic attack trying to get ready.

They needed blood for the vampires. Nectar for the tiny fairies. Vegetarian cuisine for the Fae. A hundred barrels of mulled mead had been imported for the delegation of dwarves, and that was on top of the other spirits brought in for the rest of them.

The premise was simple. Unify the leaders of each kingdom, and the rest of their people would fall in line. The only problem? Historically speaking, these people had spent a lot more time trying to kill each other than they had walking hand in hand.

A hundred barrels of mulled mead might be underestimating things...

"Morning, Hastings."

Katerina flashed a bright smile at the guard standing by the outer doorway. Even though the sun was beating down he was standing in full armor, from his boots to the tip of his spear.

"Good morning, Your Majesty." He returned the smile tenfold, a few wisps of graying hair blowing past the deep crinkles by his eyes. "Defied the maids again, did we?"

She pulled up short, one foot freezing mid-air. "How could you possibly know that?"

He chuckled. "Castle gossip travels fast. You used to know that. Must be one of those things you forgot when you were out there on the road..."

The foot came down and Katerina laughed softly. Paul Hastings was one of the few people around the castle with whom she could actually be herself. He'd been around since she was just a baby. Long enough that rank ceased to matter, and she regarded him as more of a friend.

"I hear it's supposed to be really hot today," she countered, gesturing to the heavy metal plating covering two-thirds of his body. "Fingers crossed, huh?"

It was his turn to laugh. A loud rumbling laugh that came from deep in his chest. "Yes, Milady. Fingers crossed."

She left with a sarcastic salute and took off across the lawns, dodging carts of whiskey and children draped with garlands along the way. It was one of the best things about the dress. It didn't immediately give her away. When her bright hair was pulled back, like it was today, she could pass as a wealthy villager or a lady of the court. It wasn't until the second glace that the people bustling around her recognized their own queen.

"Morning, Martin."

Martin O'Leary. One of the gypsies tasked with musical entertainment and another friend. A tall man, he glanced over his shoulder then lowered his gaze quite a bit to level upon the queen.

"Kat! Still dressing ourselves, are we?"

What is this, published somewhere?!

She ignored his question and countered with one of her own. "Have you seen Dylan?"

It was one of the things she liked most about the gypsies. They believed in friendship, not fealty. In honor, not flags. Titles were irrelevant. First names would always suffice.

"Not since last night." He finished hoisting up a beam for the stage, then turned around with a sly smile. "I figured you might have seen him between now and then."

It was one of the things she liked least about gypsies. That pesky tendency to tell the truth.

"I have no idea what you're talking about," Katerina snarked.

One of the worst-kept secrets in the five kingdoms was that she and Dylan had fallen in love. Perhaps the second-worst-kept secret was that they were completely unable to keep their hands off one another.

"At any rate, you hardly have time to go looking," he continued, speaking with a lilting accent that at times was hard to understand. "The first of the emissaries is due to arrive any..."

He trailed off, staring at her with pity. The young queen's eyes had strayed to the far edge of the clearing. Where a group of men was tearing a pair of giant cages to the ground.

Kailas' hounds.

They hadn't been seen since the battle to take back the kingdom. Rumor had it, the beasts had taken flight the second Alwyn drew his last breath. After the fighting had stopped Katerina had sent a battalion into the woods to find them, but with no luck.

Not that anyone particularly *wanted* to find them. What did you do after successfully hunting down a rogue hell hound? The truth? You probably died.

"Katerina."

The queen snapped back to the present, blinking her wide eyes as Martin stared back at her with a kind smile. He gave her a quick squeeze on the shoulder before guiding her eyes to the gate.

"It looks like the first of your friends has arrived."

Katerina whirled around with breathless anticipation, standing on her toes to see. For a minute, all she saw was the drawbridge. Then a lone rider on a dark horse came flying out of the trees. He streaked across the bridge and came to a stop in front of the main gate, leaping gracefully from the horse and shaking out his long dark hair.

The queen's eyes lit up when she saw him. Feeling like a part of her had finally come home.

Aidan.

Chapter 2

"Aidan!"

Katerina shouted loudly as she raced across the grass. Not the most queen-like display, but it'd been a long time since the kingdom had a monarch who was a teenager. Let alone one who was willing to show even a shred of human emotion.

"Aidan!"

She might have been able to surprise Dylan on a perfect day, but never Aidan. It didn't matter he had his vampire's heightened senses, the two were connected in other ways.

He looked up as she raced across the grass and watched her, a small smile playing about his lips. In the beginning, he'd found her exuberance downright suspicious. Now, it was a point of great endearment. That smile grew bigger the closer she got. By the time she leapt into the air and threw her arms around his neck, he was openly laughing.

"Now *that's* a welcome!"

His eyes were sparkling and his face was flushed—he must have fed recently. Other than that, he looked exactly as the princess remembered. Tall, pale, and entirely too handsome for his own good.

"I missed you," she murmured, squeezing him tighter. She had recently grown spoiled by making friends gifted with supernatural strength. When she leapt, they caught her. When she held on, so did they—letting her feet dangle in the air. "Please, don't go away again."

It had only been a few weeks, but the queen would swear it felt much longer. Aidan left not long after the battle, to prepare his own kind for the *things to come*. At the time, Katerina hadn't known exactly what he'd meant. But the vampire had a way of intuiting these things. The same way that Cassiel and Sera, the other immortal members of their party, had a strange way of blending the present, the future, and the past.

"I missed you, too." He held on tight. Much tighter than he allowed himself to hold most people. Then set her gently back on her feet. "You have no idea."

It was only then that Katerina saw the physical toll behind the words. Saw the faint marks of a scuffle. The outlines of cuts and bruises not fully healed.

"What happened to you?" She pulled back with a sudden frown, holding both sides of his face as she looked him up and down. "Did someone... Aidan, what could have possibly hurt you enough that it wasn't healed by blood?"

"Could you lower your voice?" He flashed a tight smile at the castle representatives making their way across the grass. "Act like a queen, not my mother."

Katerina's eyes cooled with a sarcastic smile, but she did as he asked. She even released his face, though she refused to abandon the question.

"What happened to you?" she pressed quietly, maintaining an outward calm. "Did the others do this? On that note," her eyes scanned the trees behind him, "where are the others? Weren't they supposed to be coming with you?"

Aidan tensed, so discreetly his friend didn't even notice. By the time she looked back, he was all smiles. "Oh, you of little faith. They're coming. It'll just be a few more days."

"Oh. Good." She had to admit, as curious as she was to meet Aidan's kinsfolk she was just as grateful for the stall. The arrival of a vampire delegation was the single biggest source of apprehension for those waiting back at the palace. Not only because vampires had cultivated a rather fearsome reputation, a reputation that Katerina had learned firsthand was based in truth, but because there was a lot on the table. If negotiations went south, they had no way of predicting how the vampires might respond.

"What's the matter, Kat?" As usual, Aidan guessed her every thought. He didn't need their special connection to do that. "Got something on your mind?"

She flushed, but gave him an innocent smile. "Not at all."

"It's in my head." He tapped his temple with a slender finger.

"Your travels have made you paranoid."

"Right." He laughed again then lifted an unexpected hand to her face, those dark eyes of his softening with tender affection. "I really did miss you."

Something in his voice caught her off guard. A sort of longing she didn't understand. Her eyes fixed curiously on his face and she was about to ask the question, when a loud voice called from somewhere just over her shoulder.

"Ambassador Dorsett!"

Katerina and Aidan turned at the same time. They stared for a moment, then she frowned.

"...who is he calling?"

There was a beat of silence.

"Are you serious?"

She gave Aidan a blank stare as he looked down in utter disbelief. After studying her eyes for a moment, searching for a lie, he threw back his head with a sudden laugh.

"That's me, you unbelievable spaz. Aidan *Dorsett*." Her mouth dropped in astonishment, and he laughed all over again. "What, you didn't think vampires had last names?"

"I never thought about it," she admitted. In truth, she didn't know a single immortal who considered them worth the hassle. "If you did, I would have guessed something scary. Blackthorn, or Nightshade. Or maybe like... *Deathshadow*."

She was especially pleased with the last one.

A strained silence fell between them. A silence that made the queen rethink the wisdom of antagonizing someone with fangs. Then a slow smile spread up the side of his face.

"...Deathshadow?"

"Aidan Deathshadow," she announced proudly. "It has a suitably ominous ring."

He shook his head, raking back his raven hair as the castle representatives sent to greet him drew ever closer. "And to think, these lunatics made you their queen."

She opened her mouth to reply, then shut it with a suspicious frown. "Dylan says the same thing to me almost every day."

Aidan laughed again, loosening his travelling cloak and throwing it over the back of his horse. He seemed to be reanimating the longer he was away from the rest of his kind and back in the company of friends. Like someone lost in a dark hibernation slowly coming back to life. "I bet he does. And how is our reluctant king?"

Her lips twisted up in a sly grin. "You'd know better than me."

Several months back, in the jungle swamps of the Kreo, Katerina had been attacked by a wizard disguised as a panther. Just your average Tuesday afternoon. Aidan had fought the beast off, but lost over half his blood in the process. Since Aidan and the then-princess had already bonded a little too close for comfort, her boyfriend had volunteered a vein instead.

It was a memory they'd both rather forget.

"Experiencing some unwanted side-effects, is he?" the vampire teased. "Hears himself calling out my name?"

The bond between them wasn't quite so personal. Since only Dylan had shared his blood, it was one-sided. Still, it was a level of intimacy that neither man was comfortable with just yet.

"Don't flatter yourself, vampire," Katerina scoffed. "As it turns out, we didn't even know your full name." She came to a sudden pause. "Although he did admit to having a dream about you a few nights ago. Said the two of you were in the forest, and you were teaching him how to make soup." She cocked her head with a crooked smile. "What do you suppose that means?"

Aidan rolled his eyes with a grin. "It just means that your boyfriend is even more warped than I gave him credit for." He stifled a quiet sigh as the royal envoys swept forward. "At any rate, I'd be the last person in the world who knew how to make soup..."

"Ambassador."

A trio of tall men in heavy robes swept forward. Each taking care to shake his hand. Each looking very impressed with themselves for doing so.

Katerina fought back a smile as Aidan made a conscious effort not to roll his eyes.

"We are truly honored by your presence." It was the head of the queen's own council, Abel Bishop. A man who was well-intentioned, if not exactly kind. "Chambers have been prepared for you in the east wing. I'd be happy to escort you there myself."

"That's all right," Aidan replied quickly. "I remember the way."

"I insist." The councilman smiled, either reluctant to let a vampire wander about the castle, or truly as honored as he said. "Please—allow me." He gestured to the main entrance, leaving his reluctant guest no choice.

Katerina looked on sympathetically and was about to follow along, when Aidan waved her off with a dismissive smile.

"Go find Dylan. You're out here looking for him, right?"

A regular mind reader. Sometimes she wondered if vampires were telepathic.

"Not that it's doing me any good." Her eyes swept briefly across the miniature village being erected on the castle lawns. "With my luck he's already shifted, and while the rest of us are suffering through this intolerable thing he'll be happily chasing pigeons in the woods."

Aidan chuckled softly before his eyes fluttered shut. When they opened just a moment later, they were tight with a sympathetic frown. "Actually, I suspect he's with Atticus." His eyes drifted towards the castle. "Feels like he's having a... difficult conversation."

Difficult. Katerina hung her head with a sigh. Yes, she imagined it was.

With a half-hearted wave she bid farewell to the party and trudged back up the drawbridge by herself, off to find him. It wasn't hard to do. The delegation of shifters had been meeting in one of the large ballrooms since they rejoined their king just a week before. While Dylan wasn't required to attend each of the general meetings, he was often found consulting with Atticus, his most trusted advisor, in the private chambers adjacent to the main hall.

Sure enough, the second Katerina drew close she heard the sound of arguing voices. She lingered in the hallway with bated breath. Listening on the other side of the door.

"—for the last time, Atticus, this isn't up for discussion! My personal life is my own. If you think for one second I would have come back to Belaria if I'd known this might happen—"

Katerina hung her head with a silent sigh. She'd always liked Atticus. From the very first moment he tried to help free them from the Belarian dungeons all those months ago, to the moment he took an arrow in the shoulder to save his king in the battle shortly after. He was a good man. If she was being honest, most of the representatives who'd started trickling into the castle for the summit were good men. But Atticus, like the rest of the High Kingdom, had subtly changed...

The argument sounded like a bad breakup.

"Listen," Atticus tried to temper him, "it's not you—it's us. The Council. We're just not ready for something like this yet."

"I couldn't give a *damn* what the Council is ready for."

"When you took up the crown, it came with a certain expectation. Where you would live, how you would rule... the woman you would marry."

"Mind your words carefully, Atticus. I won't give you another warning."

"We're not saying you need to break off contact," the councilman rallied desperately. "The two of you can still be friends—"

It was at that point that Dylan started yelling, and Katerina retreated back down the hall, heading to the weapons room for practice. Yes, the *weapons* room. The princess who left was not the queen who returned. People would just have to get used to it and adjust. Heaven knew she'd adjusted herself. Life since returning to the castle had been an endless series of such adjustments...

"Gentlemen, may I have the room?"

The soldiers who'd been sharpening their spears cleared out in a hurry, murmuring words of respect and casting secret glances over their shoulders as their young queen waited patiently behind them, then shut the door. The second they were gone and she was alone, the gloves came off.

"HI-YA!

With a running leap, she took down the mannequin standing closest to her. The two that were standing behind it were the next to go. She flew through the air like she'd been gifted wings, wrapping her legs around the suits of armor and twisting them effortlessly to the floor.

These particular figurines were supposed to be used specifically for weapons training. Built to withstand the attack of a thousand blades. But Katerina wasn't feeling particularly partial to the rules that morning. She'd rather rip the things apart with her bare hands.

That dragon has been lying dormant too long...

When she'd first arrived back at the castle, stumbling down from the rain-soaked roof with the remains of her multi-cultured army by her side, it had been assumed that things would pick up right where they had left off. That she would return to a life of feminine leisure. Riding, sewing, preening, playing cards. On occasion she would attend meetings of the Great Council, during which she'd be expected to remain mostly silent and adhere to the wisdom of men. Swords would be replaced with a scepter. Her army for a horde of ladies-in-waiting, ready to heed her every call.

The reality had been somewhat different.

The first thing the queen had done after her coronation was to disband the old council entirely—all those men who had failed to see that her brother was being poisoned, that an evil wizard was really the one calling the shots. They were replaced with people she trusted. Both men and women who might not have fit the traditional rank of someone permitted to set foot in the castle, but had been elevated all the same.

She had tacticians, economists, cultural liaisons, farmers, military men. She'd even brought in a locally renowned teacher from one of the smaller villagers, who was doing amazing work with children. Even her second in command, Abel Bishop. While she might not want to share a meal with the man, he had one of the greatest political minds she had ever seen.

The group was as capable as it was diverse. A brilliant cross-section of the population that she could be proud of assembling. They argued and bickered. Held great debates and heated discussions on the parliamentary floor. Great pieces of legislation had already been passed. Despite the multiple viewpoints, the kingdom was slowly entering an age of prosperity the likes of which had never been seen. But on one solitary subject, the entire conclave was in perfect accord.

Katerina Damaris must put away the girl from the forest and take her place as queen.

That didn't just mean taking up the crown. That didn't just mean sitting on the throne and guiding her people as she'd dreamed of doing for so long. It meant giving things up as well.

No more midnight rides through the forest without an escort of at least forty guards. No more playing about as a dragon in cloudy skies where she thought no one could find her. No more secret liaisons with her boyfriend, who happened to be suffering under the weight of his own crown.

Weapons were to be worn only by the people protecting her. Corsets were to be laced up tight. And the first order of business? To find a suitable husband, of course.

It was an ongoing battle. One she was vaguely aware each of her friends was fighting at the same time. A cold war between the traditions of the past and the bright promise of the future. Each one tangling together in the present. Each one refusing to give an inch.

Dylan was hearing it today. She'd most likely be hearing it tomorrow.

A wave of fire shot from her hands, hitting the center of a target mounted on the wall. It was a perfect shot. Scorching only the very center of the bullseye. After reveling for a moment, she turned to the rest of them and repeated the action seven more times.

Then the tapestries caught fire. Then she bowed her head, and trudged towards the water bucket mounted on the wall.

Maybe we should just tell them, she thought miserably. *Maybe we were wrong to keep it to ourselves, and we should just tell them.*

She had revisited the memory a thousand times. Playing it back with perfect detail.

The way the group of friends had unintentionally gathered in the hallway—each drawn out by the magic of her mother's fiery pendant. The way the stone had led them deep into the castle, revealing a secret chest hidden inside one of the walls.

The sound of Tanya's voice when she'd read the prophecy. The look on Dylan's face when those diamond rings had tumbled out into his hand.

"Put it back," he'd said suddenly. So suddenly that he'd startled the rest of them. In a flash, he was stuffing the chest back into the wall—hiding those rings forever. "Just put it back."

Cassiel had stopped them, intercepting the box with a cautious hand.

"It's unwise to ignore a prophecy," he murmured, slipping back into a slightly older way of speech. "Each one is made for a reason."

Dylan tried to grab it back, a quiet panic lighting the back of his eyes. "This one was made to make our lives a lot harder—trust me. Just put it back."

But the rest of them weren't so sure. Rather, they weren't able to do much besides stare at the tiny box as though the wood itself had come to life.

Five kingdoms to stand through the flood

Well, that's got to be the five of us, right? Men, shifters, vampires, Kreo, and Fae?

United by marriage, united by blood

Okay, that makes things a little more complicated...

Protected through grace, as only one can

Well, that's the amulet, isn't it?

To take up the crown, either woman or man

By that point, she was puzzled. Most of them had already taken up their crowns. The ones who hadn't were just waiting on logistical technicalities. The people of their realms had been hunted and scattered through decades of war. They weren't going to reassemble overnight.

Yes, the unification through marriage makes things more difficult. She shifted uneasily, shooting secret glances at the others. *Not to mention the unification through blood.*

Her friends seemed to share the same sentiment but, as it turned out, Dylan wasn't worried about the rings at all. He was worried about something else instead.

"What does it mean... the flood?"

Katerina's mind raced back to the beginning of the prophecy. Important as it might be, she'd quite overlooked that part. She'd been too distracted by the diamonds sparkling in his hand.

"Five kingdoms to stand through the flood," he repeated, casting an anxious glance up the hallway to make sure they were still alone. "I know a bit about prophecies, too, Cass, and I know that they happen in their own time. We found this *now*. After Alwyn. So what's the flood?"

The fae stared back at him, but had no response. The others were less convinced.

"It *has* to mean Alwyn," Tanya countered, grabbing the box for herself and turning it over in her hands. "His defeat ended the bloodshed and brought together each of our people. It was the greatest unifying disaster since Katerina's power-crazed ancestors seized control in the first place, and that was hundreds of years ago. No offense," she added, seeing the look on the princess' face.

"None taken."

Everything the shape-shifter was saying technically made sense, but the more Katerina thought about it, the more she saw that growing look of concern clouding the face of the man she loved, and the more she was suddenly terrified he was right.

They hadn't been unified when they fought Alwyn—they didn't have men on their side. And they certainly hadn't done it married *or* unified by blood. Only she and Dylan had shared enough blood to establish a connection. And this crown to take up? One single crown? What was that?

"We can't tell them," Aidan said softly. "If this isn't referring to the past, if this 'flood' is something still yet to come... we can't tell the rest of the people. Not yet."

Dylan nodded soundly and tried to take the box back from Tanya. Tried and failed.

"You guys are being ridiculous," she insisted. "We *just* put down our swords. Lay all these problems to rest. Now you're saying there's some other big evil out there coming to get us?"

"Not necessarily," Cassiel replied quietly, his dark eyes locked on the silent scuffle happening over the chest. "The flood could refer to anything. And the prophecy might not even be referring to us. Perhaps it's intended for some later generation. Distant descendants of the present throne."

There was a moment of silence. A fleeting moment where everyone dared to hope.

"But *we* found it." Katerina's hand drifted up to the amulet shining around her neck. "My mother's necklace led us here. *All* of us."

Her eyes drifted around the stricken circle. From Cassiel and Serafina, pale and beautiful, standing side by side. To Kailas, standing on the periphery of the circle, to Tanya's signature defiance, to Aidan's trouble eyes.

She came to rest on the man she counted on to solve every problem. The charismatic ranger who'd saved the five kingdoms just to present on a platter to the woman who'd stolen his heart.

For once, he wasn't looking back at her. His eyes were locked on the chest. Staring with such piercing intensity she'd swear he could see the diamonds glittering inside.

Five kingdoms to stand through the flood...

The decision was made. The box was hidden away. Not back in the wall, but deep inside Katerina's own chambers. Locked in a drawer where she took it out and looked at it from time to time. They would not be telling their advisors. They would not be sharing the troubling news with the people. Not until they knew what it was. Not until they'd found a way to make peace.

"Fear can be a powerful motivator," Aidan had once told her. They had been standing on the balcony, looking up at the stars. "It can bring people together. Make them unite."

The breeze picked up and he paused, gazing out over the land.

"But it won't be enough to keep them. When the fear has passed, those bonds will break."

The wise words were as true then as they were now. A lasting peace had to be made *before* the people felt pressured to make it happen. That foundation had to be laid for the right reasons, otherwise it would splinter and break. Leaving a land divided. A realm poised to fall.

We won't tell them, Katerina thought to herself, gazing bleakly at the smoking tapestries. *We'll get through these Accords and let the kingdoms unify on their own. The fate of the entire world may rest upon it.*

...no pressure.

"Milady?"

The servant's voice again. The one that seemed to haunt her every step.

"I'm sorry to interrupt, milady, but the rest of the delegations have started to arrive."

The young queen stood there quietly as the footsteps faded away down the hall. Then she doused the curtains, pulled in a deep breath, and strode with determination to the door.

Here goes nothing. Showtime.

Chapter 3

The morning after the bloodbath battle on the castle lawn, Katerina felt as though her world had come to a sudden pause. She got out of bed with no clear agenda. There was no smoky campfire or the looming promise of a sixteen-hour hike. No pressing time-crunch, or thrill of dread every time she dared to glance over her shoulder. Everything was strangely suspended. Like a waking dream.

Instead of scouting for royal soldiers, she slipped into a silk bathrobe. Instead of skinning a squirrel to roast over the fire, she went downstairs for Champagne and pastries. Her return to the castle was perfect in theory, but no matter what she tried the reality didn't seem to fit.

Her clothes were too confining. The chairs too soft.

Only one thing in her world remained constant, when everything else had flipped abruptly on its head. Only one thing remained exactly the same. Her circle of friends.

Friends who were having an even harder time adjusting to their new lives.

Dylan may have been born in a palace himself, but he had long since forsaken it for a life of adventure in the wild. Everything about the castle seemed to set him off. From the utensils, to the mirrors, to the adoring nobility that insisted on bowing to him wherever he went. Cassiel and Serafina were royalty themselves, but one had spent the better part of a century whoring about the five kingdoms, while the other had spent the last two years starving in a dungeon.

Both Aidan and Tanya were accustomed to living in the shadows, societally shamed for the particular brand of magic that ran in their veins, and Kailas? There wasn't a man, woman, or child in the five kingdoms the crown prince hadn't personally harmed.

In the days after the battle, the seven friends had clung to one another. Sleeping in adjoining rooms. Wandering like a closed unit amongst the grounds. Never more than a stone's throw away.

But such a thing could only last for so long.

Aidan left first. He felt compelled to. According to him, their victory had opened only a brief window in which things might actually be able to change. Seven days after they'd finished scrubbing the blood off the parapet, he leapt onto a borrowed horse and vanished into the forest. Tanya left soon after, having received a fearsome message from her grandmother threatening bodily harm if she didn't return to 'get things in order.' Cassiel and Serafina were the next to go, off to seek out what remained of their own people. To rally the masses and see what remained.

In the end, only Dylan remained. Granted, he did so in spite of every effort to pry him away. His advisors begged and pleaded for the better part of a month, before realizing that their king was not only happy and safe but also impossibly stubborn. They left with a promise to soon return.

The months since had been peppered with sporadic news. The occasional raven or travel-weary messenger as all the friends felt the absence in their own way.

But all of that was soon to change.

The Accords might have presented an impossible challenge—uniting the free peoples of the world under a single banner of peace. But at least they had one thing going for them.

Everyone is coming home!

Katerina saw the caravan from the northern tower, kept her eye on it as she raced full-speed towards the stairs. It was hard to make out individual faces from such a distance, but the carriages bore the silver banners of the Fae. The second they cleared the trees, a white-haired man riding near the front put on a burst of speed—shooting towards the castle with a blinding smile.

Cassiel!

This time, Katerina kept the excited shouting inside her head as she flew past the guards and skidded to a stop at the end of the drawbridge. The Fae weren't exactly partial to grand displays of emotion, and she didn't want to imagine the look on Cassiel's face if she were to bear-hug him in front of the rest of his dignified party.

That being said, it took her by complete surprise when he leapt gracefully off his stallion and swept her up in the world's biggest embrace.

"Kat!"

His strong arms wrapped around her slender body as he lifted her clean off the ground, completely oblivious to the fact that her feet were dangling somewhere around his shins. She let out a gasp of shock, then threw her arms around his neck. Breathing in the familiar scent. Grinning ear to ear. Choking on mouthfuls of silky white-blonde hair.

"Don't. Ever. Leave. Again." She squeezed him even tighter, giving him the exact same command she'd given to Aidan just an hour before. "Please, Cass. I don't know what you were thinking, leaving Dylan and me unsupervised, but it must absolutely *never* happen again!"

He threw back his head with a sparkling laugh, a sound that warmed her from the inside out. "I'm sure you two found ways to pass the time." He set her on her feet with a twinkling smile. "Speaking of which, where is my best friend?"

A bloody good question.

Attendance was mandatory for the 'greeting of the delegations,' and Katerina had warned her boyfriend five times the previous evening not to be late. Then again, said boyfriend had never placed a high priority on mandatory attendance...

"Oh, you know Dylan," she stalled, glancing back towards the castle. "Probably making sure that everything is set up for the banquet. I'm sure he'll be here any minute."

Unfortunately, he *did* know Dylan. That was the problem.

"Katerina," he said sternly, "I count on you to look after him when I'm away. This close to any major life event, you should be keeping him on a leash—"

"Cass!"

The pair turned around as Aidan swept forward with a smile. Though he and the fae had never bonded as well as the rest they embraced warmly, pulling back with matching smiles.

"When did you get here?"

"Only an hour ago." The vampire's eyes flickered to the castle as he stifled a shudder. "And I've spent over half the time since trying to return a live goat that was delivered to my room."

Cassiel chuckled, while Katerina clapped a hand over her eyes. Never before had the castle entertained such a diverse group of people. Their 'vampire protocol' needed a little work.

"What about the rest of your party?" Cassiel asked, glancing up at the castle as the rest of his own delegation made their way across the bridge. "Do they have everything they need?"

For the second time, Aidan shifted uncomfortably. A momentary lapse before a quick smile.

"They're not here yet—got delayed on the road. It should be just a few more days."

Katerina and Cassiel looked up with the same question, then decided not to ask. Truth be told, they didn't want to imagine what might delay a large group of vampires.

"Well, perhaps it's better if they miss the opening feast anyway," the fae teased. "We wouldn't want them getting any ideas. At any rate, it gives us more time to—"

"My lord."

The three friends turned around to see a stately-looking fae descending from a nearby carriage. While the Fae were an eternal people, blessed with immortal life, there was something particularly aged about this man. He moved with a slow, dignified grace. And although he was clearly much older than his prince, he was regarding Cassiel with a look of sheer adoration.

That's the first thing Katerina noticed.

The second thing was that he was carrying a truly enormous white bird.

What the—?

She and Aidan took a giant step back while Cassiel took a faltering step forward, staring between the man and the bird with a look of true astonishment.

"Leonor... what is this?"

The man offered a fleeting smile, his eyes shining with devotion. "I had hoped there would be a better place to do it, but we are left with few options and less time. The Council wished to wait until the Accords, and this is not something that can be done in the halls of men." He held out the arm with the bird as those gathered behind him bowed their heads with respect. "We present this to you, my prince. A token of our esteem and appreciation. A gift from the Fae to the House of Elénarin. We thank you, Cassiel. For everything you have done."

Well, that was... unexpected.

Katerina and Aidan blinked in surprise, then turned to Cassiel. But for the first time since she had met him, her eloquent friend was speechless. He simply stared, at a loss for words.

After a few seconds there was some quiet laughter from the delegation of Fae, and the old man stepped forward with a kind smile, placing the bird gently in his arms.

"Your parents would be proud."

Cassiel bowed his head, parting his lips with an uncertain response. In the end, he merely nodded. The man left with a deferential nod, and just moments later the entire delegation was heading into the castle, leaving the three friends standing alone on the bridge.

Along with the giant bird.

They stood there quietly. Staring as the caravan vanished behind the castle gate. Then Aidan glanced up at the bird with the hint of a frown.

"...they kept that stashed in the carriage this entire time?"

Katerina elbowed him in the ribs, keeping all related questions carefully to herself. This was clearly an important moment in Cassiel's life, and she didn't want to ruin it by asking if his magical new pet would require some dead rats from the kitchen.

Instead, she cleared her throat and forced a casual smile. "So, uh... what are you supposed to do with it?"

The mystical creature had folded its ten-foot wingspan and was curled up tranquilly in Cassiel's arms. Resting its head against his chest, like it was on the verge of falling asleep.

"Now?" Cassiel's eyes were still locked upon the castle. "I'm supposed to snap its neck."

There was a beat of silence.

"What?"

"Wait—*what*?"

She and Aidan whirled around, feeling unexpectedly protective of the strange creature, but Cassiel was already walking away. A faint grin flickering in his eyes.

"The two of you are hopeless. It's almost too easy..."

They stared in open-mouthed shock as he disappeared into the castle as well before hurrying to compose themselves. Each unwilling to look the other in the eye.

"I didn't believe him," Katerina said stiffly.

"Neither did I."

IF THE CASTLE HAD BEEN in a controlled panic attack that morning, it had escalated into full chaos by the time the three friends got inside. The staff was openly hyperventilating, the ice sculptures were starting to melt, and people were rushing by at such manic speeds that no one even stopped to acknowledge the esteemed trio as they made their way slowly up the stairs.

"This is great," Aidan said cheerfully. A gifted flask of blood from the kitchens had greatly improved his mood after getting nipped in the shoulder by Cassiel's bird. "Complete anonymity. A far cry from the infernal spotlight they had me under this morning."

He had a point. It was a testament to how frantic everyone was that no one had yet to mention the giant bird feasting on the floral arrangements while nestled in the fae's arms.

"I don't know what you mean," Cassiel replied stiffly. "I think it's a disgrace."

Katerina rolled her eyes, trudging up past a group of shifty-eyed goblins. "You're just saying that because the kitchens didn't have that weird flower drink you wanted. And you have yet to explain your new spirit animal, by the way."

As if on cue, the bird flapped away from him and landed on the bannister post a few stairs up, surveying the bustling castle as if the entire celebration was in honor of itself.

"What's the point? You wouldn't understand." Cassiel lifted his chin haughtily as a cluster of maids went tearing past him. "Vampires are inherently uncivilized, and you, Katerina, have all the maturity of a drunken child."

She paused mid-step and shot him a withering glare. "You'd better come up with something a *little* better than that when you introduce me at the banquet tonight."

"I'm not introducing you."

"You are now."

"Yeah," Aidan let out a contended sigh, "I've missed this."

"I will *not* be introducing you, and that's final." The fae snapped his fingers for the bird as they climbed past it, heading towards the eastern hall. "It's bad enough you have my delegation seated next to a contingent of dwarves—"

There was a blur of color then he slammed into the wall, a lusty maid pressed to his chest.

"What—?"

"Oh, pardon me," she interrupted, batting her long eyelashes while gazing up at him with a sultry smile. "Must have tripped on my own shoes."

Tripped on my own shoes. That's a new one.

Over the course of their travels, Katerina had seen each of the men fall victim to such advances many times before. Dylan had gotten cornered by a star-struck shifter when they were returning to their room in Pora, and Aidan had been propositioned so many times the rest of them had quite simply lost count. It wasn't really their fault. They were as the heavens made them.

That being said, this particular encounter was slightly more forward than the rest.

"Girl," Katerina chided quietly, "be on your way."

The maid ignored her completely, staring dreamily into Cassiel's eyes. Her fingers tightened on the front of his shirt, and if Katerina wasn't mistaken she leaned in for a quick sniff.

"The staff at the castle has been getting ready for the summit for weeks. We servants have been ordered to accommodate your every need." She wet her lips ever so casually and stretched up onto her toes. "Your *every* need, my lord."

While he was usually patient with such advances, this one crossed a line. Cassiel's eyes flashed with scarcely contained rage as he took her wrists, prying them away from his body.

"Take your hands off me, and be gone." He spoke with a tone that sent chills careening down Katerina's spine. "I'm sure you have things to clean."

Aidan smothered a smile and Katerina almost felt sorry for the girl. She knew firsthand how terrifying her friend could be. But instead of backing down, the maid leaned even closer.

"Are you sure? I could make it worth your while—"

WHAT?!

Katerina let out a gasp, and Cassiel looked like he was on the verge of abandoning decorum and summoning his bird to swallow her whole—when there was a shimmer of air and the maid disappeared with a cheerful *pop*. A gorgeous shape-shifter appeared in her wake. Grinning from ear to ear.

"Nicely handled. Though I would have appreciated a bit of profanity."

The others let out a burst of laughter as Cassiel froze where he stood. His lips parted in delayed shock, but by the time his girlfriend kissed him he was already starting to smile.

"I have *begged* you to stop doing that."

She dropped back to her feet as he peeled himself ruefully off the wall. "Yes, but that's something you should know about me by now." Her eyes sparkled with a roguish wink. "I happen to *love* it when you beg."

"Too much information," Aidan murmured.

The shifter jumped on him next, ignoring his general 'no touching' rule as she tried her best to ruffle his elegant waves of hair. She saved the queen for last, embracing her like a sister.

"I'm never leaving again!"

"Never leave me again!"

They cried out at the same time, then laughed as they echoed each other's words. Despite the sudden change in rank and position, they'd always be the two girls who met out in the woods.

Trapped on the world's worst camping trip.

"So how about it, Kat?" Tanya draped an arm over her shoulder, leaving all the laws of protocol and propriety behind. "You been keeping my throne warm for me?"

Katerina rolled her eyes as the nearest stationed guards looked up in alarm. "I told you to stop saying stuff like that in the castle. They take jokes like that seriously around here."

"I'm not joking at all. I fully plan to assassinate you and seize the crown for myself."

"Don't you have a crown of your own?" Aidan prompted teasingly.

"Yeah, but you've met my grandmother." Tanya stretched her arms with a yawn. "The thing's made of cedar bark and bones."

"You've got to get changed, my love." Cassiel flipped the edge of her travelling cloak with a fond grin. "The banquet's going to be starting soon."

She gave him a shameless grin, unwilling to part after so long a separation. "Care to give me a hand? You know I can never get all those little buttons by myself."

He took an automatic step towards her, eyes dancing with mischief, then glanced quickly about the castle and took a step back. "I... shouldn't. Not here." Her hands planted firmly on her hips, and he gave her a swift kiss on the forehead. "Later—I promise."

Then, before she could make a scene, he turned to Katerina with a distraction. "You'd better go find Dylan. With our luck he's already shifted and—"

"—and is chasing a bunch of pigeons in the woods." She nodded wearily. "Yeah, I know."

With a quick wave she hurried off, just as the shifter registered Cass' new pet for the first time.

"So you like birds, huh?"

WHEN YOU'RE ABOUT TO host an international peace summit and have a castle full of guests, the last thing you want to do is climb to the top of the northern tower and take off your clothes. But that's exactly what Katerina found herself doing, just as the sun dipped below the trees.

Cass was right, she grumbled to herself as she dropped her dress to the floor. *I should have put him on a leash...*

She hardly even paused before she leapt out of the highest window in the castle. Hardly gave the ground a second glance as she closed her eyes and lifted her arms above her head. There was a stirring in the air around her, a deep blossom of heat that radiated out of her chest.

A second later, a giant crimson dragon was rising into the sky. Shooting plumes of fire as it whipped about in the air.

This is more like it. This is what I've been missing.

The Council of the High Kingdom hadn't exactly tried to ban her from shifting. Quite the contrary, it was widely acknowledged that if it weren't for that particular skill, the battle with Alwyn would have been lost and most of them would have been in a mass grave somewhere in the forest.

That being said, she wasn't exactly encouraged to shift either.

When Katerina had made the monumental decision to relinquish control and grant each of the five kingdoms autonomy, they had split into five very distinct realms. There was the kingdom of shifters, the kingdom of the Fae, the kingdom of the vampires, the kingdom of the Kreo, and the kingdom of men. Katerina, of course, was queen of the men.

But had also turned out to be... a shifter.

It was a discrepancy that no one talked about. At least, not to her face. But she'd heard them whispering about it behind closed doors. How could the blood of her mother, Adelaide Gray, have been fused with the supernatural? A woman who came from one of the oldest houses of men?

It was a question without an answer, and the whole discussion was soon laid to rest. But ever after, Katerina found that she never shifted in the open. She would do so in private, if she did so at all. Taking to the skies only on cloudy days. Returning at night when no one could see her.

All right, you little truant... where are you?

Dylan wasn't the most predictable, but in this case he wasn't that hard to find. In this case, Katerina simply aimed for the tallest turret on the highest tower. Sure enough, there he was.

Even if she was given a thousand years, it would never stop shocking her—how absolutely beautiful he was. She woke up beside him every morning, and it still took her breath away.

He was sitting with his chin resting on his hand. Eyes locked on the horizon. Lost in thought. He barely glanced up at the crimson dragon that dropped down from the sky, but offered a sweet smile to the naked girl who sat down beside him.

For a while, they didn't talk. Then she leaned over and took his hand.

"You know, everyone's gathering for the banquet downstairs."

His shoulders fell with an almost imperceptible sigh. "Yeah, I figured."

She bit her lip, shooting him a sideways glance. "Cass is here. Along with Aidan and Tanya. I think Sera's coming later tonight." This made more of an impression, but still he showed no inclination to move. The queen pursed her lips, fought back an exasperated grin, and leaned against his shoulder instead. "I hear there's going to be jousting."

"There is not."

"And gambling, and drinking, and whoring... and all those things that you love."

His lips twitched up in a grin as he shot her a sideways grin. "You think I love *whoring*?"

"They're having a parade of all my ex-boyfriends—making them march naked through the hall just so people can throw things at them and laugh."

"We don't need a feast to do that."

"And, need I remind you, this entire 'summit for peace' was technically *your* idea..."

His head bowed with a sigh and he pushed halfway to his feet. Then the sound of distant laughter echoed up from the grounds and he settled back down again, squeezing her hand. "I have an idea."

Here we go again...

"Instead of going to the banquet—"

She closed her eyes with a smile, repeating the exact lines from her dream. "—let's stay here and get naked instead?"

His eyes lit up with honest surprise as his lips curved up with a smile. "Yes, that's *exactly* what I was going to say."

Shocker.

The queen rolled her eyes, staring down at the people below. "We have got to stop spending so much time together."

He ignored her completely, pressing his advantage. "So is that a yes?"

"*No*—Dylan!" She laughed, pushing to her feet and pulling him reluctantly with her. "Now come on, we're going to be late!"

Together, the two of them shimmied down the slippery tiles and dropped down to the roof above his bedroom. From there, it was just a semi-impossible—and highly embarrassing, given that Katerina was naked—to swing through his window and into his room.

She landed lightly on the floor, fought off his immediate advances and wrapped herself tightly in his cloak, preparing to make the mad dash to her own chambers.

"Would you stop!" she giggled, tumbling out into the corridor with him hot on her heels. "I am the *queen* here, damnit! You can't just—"

She pulled him to a sudden stop, melting them back behind a suit of armor as two other voices filtered down the hall. Yet another couple having a heated discussion.

"—not trying to be unfair, I'm just telling you the way it is. Some of these people are over five hundred years old, Tanya. This... they won't understand."

"Then we'll *make* them understand," the shape-shifter replied fiercely. She must have seen the look on his face, because a second later her voice melted into softer tones. "In the meantime, we'll be careful. I promise. Come on, it's not like we're the only forbidden couple in the castle."

Katerina and Dylan shared a quick glance, then shrugged.

"We'll be casual," Tanya continued coaxingly, taking him by the hand. "We'll be discreet—"

There was a mighty crash as the suit of armor gave way, spilling the hidden couple clumsily into the hall. Tanya and Cassiel froze, staring down with identical expressions as Katerina and Dylan untangled themselves and pushed quickly to their feet. A second later they remembered his cloak, and hurried to wrap it around her naked body.

The queen winced as they straightened, while the ranger flashed his friends a hopeful smile.

"Uh... hey, guys. Glad you could make it."

For a moment, nobody moved. It was as if time had stopped moving. Then Cassiel and Tanya continued walking down the hall like nothing had ever happened.

"Like I said... *we'll* be casual. *We'll* be discreet."

Chapter 4

The dress was emerald green satin, gold brocade running down the front. The bodice had been inlaid with jewels—garnets and rubies to match her mother's fiery pendant. The crown was heavy, but by now she had gotten used to the weight. Her hair was loose and gently waved. A smear of blood-red crimson had been rubbed across her lips.

The entire look had taken no less than an hour to create. Not counting the three weeks spent by the royal seamstress. No expense had been spared. Tonight, everything had to be perfect.

And it will be. If I can ever manage to walk in these heels.

Despite the sheer tonnage of the dress, Katerina felt like she was floating as she hurried down the hall to meet her friends. The seven of them were supposed to arrive together, after the rest of the guests had already been seated. Entering as a united front. The five kingdoms together as one.

The symbolism was a bit heavy-handed, but none of them particularly cared.

It was no secret how much was riding on the success of the summit. The next era could be a time of great peace, or the peoples of the land could regress into old rivalries and bloodshed. It all depended on tonight. On the next few days. On whether or not the people gathered in the great hall could put aside their differences long enough to remember why they were there.

For a better future. For the chance of a future at all.

Again... no pressure.

She teetered down the grand staircase as best she could, only to discover that she was not the first to arrive. She was the second. And she wasn't the only one who'd gone the extra mile.

"Holy cow, Cass."

Having lived with the fae for a series of months, she was already prepared for a certain level of enchantment. But the sight of him now was enough to take anyone's breath away.

His pale skin and ivory hair shone with an ethereal glow in the light of the candles set about the entryway. The hem of his silver cloak swept lightly upon the floor. The Fae had unique a way of blending clothing and armor, and while Katerina had no name for what she was looking at it was effective nonetheless. Graceful even in stillness, she could just as easily see him upon a throne as wandering through a forest, fighting off ancient monsters using nothing but his bare hands. Only the eyes kept her grounded. There was something truly inescapable about those dark eternal eyes.

"Katerina Damaris, close your mouth. You're gawking like a peasant."

...and there's that winning personality.

She tripped down the remainder of the stairs with a glare. Wishing, just once, that *he* would do something ungainly that *she* could point to and laugh. It didn't seem likely.

"Where's Tanya?" she countered, trying to salvage what was left of her pride. "Or are you guys still in the middle of that huge relationship-ending fight we interrupted?"

He never blinked.

"You mean when I saw you naked?"

Touché.

Vowing to never engage in a verbal war of wits with a fae, the queen smiled innocently then spun around in a girlish twirl. "Well, what do you think of my dress?"

It was a laughable diversion, but bouts of sudden childlike honesty always scored big points with Cassiel. The lofty façade vanished immediately, melting into a genuinely affectionate smile as he spun her around in another twirl.

"Beautiful." His eyes twinkled and gave her a brotherly wink. "If I didn't know any better, I'd say you looked like a queen."

She glowed on the inside, and lifted a careless hand to her crown. "That's what the adoring masses tell me. At any rate, it's the only reason I'd ever wear this thing. It's heavy as he—"

"Lamenting the weight of your crown?" There was a blur of shadow, then suddenly Aidan was standing beside them. "Talk about first-world problems."

"Would you look at that?" Katerina said dryly. "A vampire with a sense of humor."

"There are nine of us," he replied seriously. "You're lucky to have met one."

She grinned in spite of herself, looking him up and down.

He hadn't come in ceremonial garb like the others. Truth be told, he wasn't dressed very differently than he did most days at all. Black shirt. Dark pants. A fitted charcoal jacket that hung perfectly on his athletic frame. It wasn't exactly formal, but it was appropriate at the same time.

Maybe it was a vampire thing. Maybe it was simply Aidan.

"You clean up nice." He flipped back one of Katerina's waves with a smile. "Nice crown."

"Yeah, I hope it's worth all the trouble we went through to get it."

The gang looked up as Tanya and Dylan sauntered into the room. One was wearing a gown of light lavender, her spikey hair streaked with ribbons of delicate crystals. The other was dressed like the world's most beautiful and petulant king. Complete with a ceremonial sword and a scowl.

At first glance, Katerina didn't understand why they were walking arm in arm. A second later, she realized that one was literally keeping the other from bolting to the door.

"I caught this one trying to sneak off to the stables," Tanya said authoritatively, tightening her vise-like grip. "Had to shift into a cave troll just to haul him back here myself."

Dylan was glaring a hole into the carpet, refusing to meet anyone's eye. "...it was terrifying."

There was a spattering of laughter as Katerina slipped her arm through his with a grin. "Did someone forget he's dating a vengeful dragon who would roast him alive if he was late for dinner?"

"...that's somehow even *more* terrifying."

Cassiel rolled his eyes in exasperation as Katerina combed back a curl of Dylan's unruly hair.

It wasn't the first time he'd tried to make himself scarce during some royal event. When a Kreo ambassador had arrived to discuss the number of seats allowed to each delegation, the king found himself taking a spur-of-the-moment hunting trip. When a trio of shifters had arrived from his own kingdom, he had fallen mysteriously ill. Katerina came to check on him later, only to find him with a bottle of whiskey in the weapon's room, happily rewinding the grip on his beloved knife.

"Look, sweetie, I know you hate things like this. I know you'd rather battle a horde of Kasi warlords than have dinner in a room full of diplomats. But you need to pull it together now, okay?"

"At least he's dressed half-appropriately," Cassiel muttered appraisingly. "I've been sending him different wardrobe options for the better part of a month."

Aidan turned away to hide his smile as Dylan looked to the heavens for strength.

"Guy still tries to babysit me from over a thousand leagues away..."

"And a good thing he does," Katerina said sternly before flashing him a sudden smile. "You look very nice, babe."

"Thanks," he muttered lifelessly. "You do... too."

His jaw dropped shamelessly and he barely managed to tag on the final word. For the first time, his eyes swept over every inch of his girlfriend. Taking in every single detail. Glowing with a fierce sort of pride that quickly turned into the predatory hunger she loved so well.

"Kat—"

"There's no time," Tanya said impatiently, smoothing down her hair as the group of them lined up at the door. "We need to get in there."

"Did none of you learn to count?"

The sudden flurry of activity came to an abrupt halt as the friends turned at the same time to the vampire standing in their midst. He was staring back with an amused smile. Arching a single eyebrow. Waiting for them to pick up on it themselves.

Katerina did a quick headcount, then turned to Cassiel with a sigh. "Where's your bloody sister?"

"Probably with your bloody brother," he snapped defensively, but his eyes flickered apologetically back to the main staircase at the same time.

The herald in the ballroom was already beginning to make their introductions, and the dignitaries were pushing noisily to their feet.

Katerina cast a wistful glance at the closed door then trudged back to the staircase with a stifled sigh, teetering precariously in her tall heels. "You guys go on ahead. It's important that at least *some* of us enter together." She gritted her teeth with a forced smile. "I'll go get Sera and Kailas."

Dylan stepped forward with a frown, ignoring the pompous baritone booming through the gilded walls. "Just come with us, Kat. It would look conspicuous if you don't. Once everyone's seated and eating, I can double back and get them myself."

"It would look *conspicuous* if I arrived and Kailas didn't," she replied, already halfway up the stairs. "You know people around the castle already look at him differently. I don't want to add fuel to the fire. *Especially* with the people in that room. Just say we're arriving late because our kingdom is hosting the event. Say there were some last-minute preparations that required our attention."

It looked like he wanted to protest, but they were out of time. The man inside was already calling out names, and the double doors opened a crack to reveal a sea of waiting faces—all of them craning to get a glimpse of the friends as they walked inside. Instead, he took his place with the others, casting one more troubled glance over his shoulder before the doors swung open and his face transformed with an instant smile.

In perfect synchronicity, the four of them entered the ballroom. Tall and gracious. Waving with charming smiles. The bright hope for the future, standing together as a united front.

The applause was deafening. It echoed in Katerina's ears as she eventually just took off her shoes and climbed back up the winding staircase. Cursing her twin with every grinding step.

Our 'perfect' night is off to a great start already...

GROWING UP IN THE CASTLE, the royal twins used to have adjoining rooms. They were each other's favorite playmates, and such proximity was conducive for building forts, or playing knights, or whatever else they had on their agenda for the day. When they grew older, they received rooms at opposite ends of the castle. Such distance was conducive for fleeing the grounds when one twin tried to kill the other under the influence of an evil spell.

After the *battle of the two dragons* (as the locals had taken to calling it), the Damaris siblings had split the distance. Katerina moved into a room in the northern tower, one that hadn't been soaked in her ladies-in-waiting's blood, and Kailas moved into the western wing. It was just a four-minute walk to each other's chambers. They could visit whenever so inclined.

They had yet to be inclined.

"Katerina, thank goodness you're here."

The queen looked up to see a real-life angel floating towards her. Flawless porcelain skin and fragile, doll-like features. A long silver dress that whispered lightly over the floor. Bright glowing eyes and clouds of billowing hair that always seemed to be blowing with its own inexplicable breeze.

And she's sweet. I freakin' hate how sweet she is.

"You look beautiful," Serafina added as the two met in the hall. "That's a lovely gown."

Case in point.

Katerina suppressed a sigh and forced a smile instead. She might not be thrilled to be living with her boyfriend's perfect ex, but what could you do? The fae was in love with her brother. And her brother was living right here. As long as that was the case, they were all one big happy family.

"So do you—look beautiful, I mean." To make matters worse, she was so intimidated by the lovely girl that she always came off like a stammering fool. "You always do, so it's no big shock."

She stopped before she could make things worse. Already, the enchanting fae was looking at her with that kind smile that always made her feel like she had something stuck to her face.

"Where's my brother?" she blurted, hurrying to get to the point. "The banquet just started and the others have already gone in."

A tiny frown creased Serafina's forehead as she glanced back towards their shared room. "That's exactly why I was coming to get you. Kailas says he isn't going to attend. He thinks the whole thing will go a lot smoother if he isn't there."

He isn't wrong.

"Well, that's..." Katerina hesitated, trying to think of a way to end the sentence without hurting the girl standing in front of her. "I mean, if he really doesn't want to go—"

"You need to change his mind," Serafina interrupted. "Convince him to come. I've said everything I can, but he needs to hear it from you. You're his sister."

Katerina's heart tightened at the word. She hadn't felt like Kailas' sister in a long time. "I'm not sure what I can say," she mumbled, hyper-aware of the fact that she was still holding her shoes. "You would have a far better chance of—"

"Just remind him of everything that's at stake." Serafina gave her a gentle push, leaving her directly in front of the door. "Of the peace this summit is trying to build."

The queen fidgeted uneasily, about to refuse, but the fae took her suddenly by the hand.

"Katerina, this isn't just about uniting the five kingdoms for Kailas. It isn't about political alliances or coalescing the realm. It's personal for him. It's the first step towards redemption."

And why should my brother's redemption have anything to do with me?

A younger version of herself might have asked the question out loud. This older version, the one who wore a crown and had a ballroom of people waiting downstairs, simply nodded.

"I'll do my best."

The Fae princess lit up with a radiant smile, then gave her an unexpected kiss on the cheek.

"You know, Dylan was right about you." She backed gracefully towards the stairs, a little twinkle dancing in her eyes. "You really were born to wear that crown."

A second later, she disappeared. Leaving Katerina feeling lost and confused. Standing outside her brother's bedroom with a pair of dangerously high heels draped over her arm.

Oh, come on! How can I hate her when she says things like that?!

Feeling both severely cheated and profoundly touched, Katerina raised her hand to knock on the door... and then slowly lowered it back to her side.

The people had believed the official statement. *Technically*. They understood that the young prince hadn't been acting of his own volition when he committed unspeakable atrocities and countless acts of genocide. *In theory*. They accepted the fact that it had been Alwyn all along. That Kailas Damaris had been under a powerful spell.

But none of that mattered. The blood of his victims still stained the streets, and technicalities didn't mean shit when you were standing in front of a grave.

The prince was reviled. People stopped talking when he entered a room. On the rare occasions he would leave the castle, they would throw things in the streets. A week after the dust had settled on the battlefield, an angry mob had swarmed the castle—demanding his head. Of course, this had prompted Serafina to threaten war with the Fae should any harm befall him.

This was news to the Fae, but they didn't dare refuse their resurrected princess any request.

In a perfect world, Katerina would be spearheading the campaign to exonerate him. Doing everything she could to help clear his name. But she found herself standing in the hallway outside his room, unable to lift her hand to knock. Eight years of cruelty didn't just vanish overnight. Some scars were past absolution, and the queen carried more than most.

It didn't help that remnants of the spell still lingered in his blood. The darkness had taken time to work its way into his system, and it would take time to fully work its way out.

The other day, Kailas had back-handed a servant who'd failed to refill his wine glass. It was a knee-jerk reaction. A dark reflex that was beyond his control. By the time his eyes cleared and he became aware of what had happened, the servant had fled from the room in tears. A week before that, he'd woken up in the dungeon—no idea of how he'd gotten there. A week before that he'd set a fire in his bedroom, just to watch it burn.

Katerina understood it was the remains of the spell. She understood that her twin brother was still in there, fighting for what was left of his soul. But the truth was as simple as it was sad.

It didn't matter.

She was afraid of him. She didn't know if she'd ever stop being afraid of him. She didn't know if she'd ever be able to knock on his door.

Fortunately, that night, she didn't have to. It opened before she could touch it.

"Sera," a soft voice called, "you forgot your—*Kat*."

He cut off suddenly, freezing in the doorway as his sister stared back with wide eyes.

The pair might have been living in the same castle for the last several weeks, but they hadn't been left alone together even a single time. Dylan would never have permitted it. Katerina would never have allowed it to happen herself. The only reason she'd volunteered to collect him for the feast was that she'd thought Serafina would be there as well.

"Uh... hi." She tucked her hair behind her ear, a nervous gesture she'd grown out of but which always seemed to come back in his presence. "I was just... you know that the banquet has started."

For his part, the prince seemed just as out of sorts himself. His voice trailed off as he lingered uncertainly in the doorway, not knowing on which side he should be.

"Yeah, about that..." He raked his fingers back through his hair, a gesture that reminded her disconcertingly of Dylan. "I think it's probably best if I don't go. Just given the general sentiment of the people and all. We want the summit to go off without a hitch, and I... would complicate that."

I'll give him this... he's depressingly self-aware.

The princess bowed her head, worrying the carpet with her toe. If she was being honest with herself, he was absolutely right. Now wasn't the time for added controversy. The next few days were going to be hard enough. At the same time, there was a chance Serafina was right, too. "Look, it's up to you," she began, unwilling to commit either way. "If you think—"

"Can't walk in your shoes, huh?"

She broke off suddenly, looking up at him in surprise. "What?"

His eyes sparkled, and for a split second she saw a hint of that boy she used to know. The one who used to come knocking at her door every time he had a nightmare. The one who used to sneak her desserts from the kitchen when she was sick in bed.

"You never could walk in heels." He gestured to the pair still dangling from her wrist. "Ever since we were kids. You could dance the Terecian waltz from the time you were six, but you never could walk in heels."

He didn't say it with any kind of agenda, and she had no idea why it hit her so hard. But in that moment, Katerina suddenly made up her mind.

"You're coming to this banquet." There wasn't an ounce of compromise in her voice. It was the voice of a sister. And a queen. "I couldn't care less about the 'general sentiment' of the people. You are the crown prince. Next in line for the throne. If business is to be conducted on behalf of the realm, then you deserve a seat at the table." She pulled in a breath. "So get dressed, Kailas."

For a moment, he simply stood there. Frozen in surprise. Staring the same way he had when she'd told him she could shift into a dragon. Then the hint of a smile flickered across his face.

"I'll just grab my coat..."

Brother and sister made their way into the banquet hall that night. Standing tall and walking side by side. Putting the past behind him, with the promise of the future shining in their eyes.

Little did they know, it was going to be a night they would never forget.

Chapter 5

There was no fanfare when Katerina and Kailas entered the ballroom. Quite the contrary, they took the herald completely by surprise. But there wasn't a person in the room who didn't freeze dead still when they saw the prince and queen standing side by side. There wasn't a single conversation that didn't screech to a halt the second they came through the door.

Men and shifters openly gawked at the siblings, craning their necks to get a better view. The table of dwarves froze with drumsticks halfway to their mouths, dripping slow stains of grease upon the table. The Fae looked offended. The Kreo were upset. An assortment of goblins actually looked a bit interested, but visibly cringed the second the prince glanced their way.

A whispered hush fell over the entire banquet, and Katerina felt her brother stiffen by her side. There was a hitch in his breathing. A nervous tremor ran through his hands. Then, just before he could panic and turn right around, the sound of slow clapping echoed through the room.

The queen froze and glanced around with the rest of them, searching for the source of the noise. Then her mouth fell open in surprise as her handsome boyfriend pushed to his feet.

There was no lost love between Dylan and Kailas. If it hadn't been for that pesky family relation, there was a chance the ranger would kill him on the spot. But if there was one thing stronger than Dylan's hatred for Kailas, it was his love for Katerina.

It was a love that knew no limits. A love that would propel him to his feet when he saw her frozen and nervous in front of a crowd. Even if that meant lifting his hands in applause. Even if it meant breaking the ice for a sworn enemy.

And that is why I love you.

At first, the crowd was as shocked as she was. Even the rest of the friends, sitting with him at the head table, had frozen in their seats, too surprised to move. Then, slowly, ever so slowly, the applause spread from person to person, filling the rest of the room.

It was a slow swell, starting with a single person at every table. That person was always quick to disappear and, judging from the fact that no one ever seemed to recognize them, Katerina suspected that Tanya was making the rounds, helping it along.

By the time she and Kailas had reached their table, nearly everyone had joined in. Making it a proper welcome. One that lasted until they nodded graciously and took their seats.

"See?" she whispered under her breath. "That wasn't so bad."

Kailas gave her a look that was torn between exasperation and intense relief before sinking back in his chair, taking Serafina's hand beneath the table. Katerina did the same. Nodding curtly to the head of her council as a hundred conversations broke out over the ballroom once more.

"Thank you for that," she murmured to Dylan. He was the first to stand and the last to take his seat. Remaining on his feet until she'd made it all the way through the crowd. "Really, I know how you feel about him. You didn't have to do all that."

"Of course I did," he answered briskly, shooting her a quick smile as he filled her glass with Champagne. "I was foolish enough to fall in love, now I must suffer the consequences."

She laughed in spite of herself, feeling significantly more relaxed now that she was no longer trapped in the spotlight with public enemy number one. "You were *foolish* enough to fall in love, huh?"

"It's brought me nothing but trouble."

"If I recall correctly it also brought you a crown, a kingdom, and a general purpose for your aimless life. But let's not split hairs..."

"No, let's not." He flashed her a dimpled grin before angling their chairs together. "So, fill me in on everything that's been happening. I'm sorry I haven't exactly... kept up with the details."

That's a generous way of putting it.

She snorted into her Champagne, then glanced around quickly to make sure nobody had seen. "*What*? You mean the great Dylan Hale isn't a party planner? And here I thought rangers were good at everything..."

"I'm trying here, Kat. Work with me."

"Okay," she ticked things off on her fingers, listing them one by one, "well, in the last week, I've liaised with nine separate diplomatic parties, settled a border dispute on the edge of the Horal Forest, pretended to speak Furgoli just so I could free up another twelve seats in this banquet hall, and had to double-plan every meal to include vegetarian options for the Fae."

She cast a quick look down the table, then lowered her voice conspiratorially.

"And speaking of... I lived in the woods with Cass for months. The man is not a vegetarian."

It certainly looked that way now. He had left the head table and was mingling politely with his own people. Chiming in to all the right conversations. Sampling the native cuisine.

"That's my fault," Dylan admitted, following her gaze. "When we first started travelling around together, he was unwilling to consider the idea of eating meat. That being said, there wasn't a lot of other food. In the end, he came to a sort of compromise—said that he wouldn't eat an animal unless it tried to eat him first."

Katerina blinked incredulously, waiting for the rest of the story.

"And, what?" she finally prompted. "*That* many things attacked you?"

"Not on their own." Dylan shot her a secret grin. "I baited the campsite."

She burst out laughing, just as Cassiel returned to the table and sat down on Dylan's other side. He poured himself a glass of wine, and turned to them with a smile.

"What are we laughing about?"

"Nothing," Dylan said quickly. "Drink more."

"Cassiel had a busy morning himself." Aidan took over narrating the day's events with his own unique style. "He'd only just gotten over the bridge when some old man threw a bird at him."

Dylan started nodding automatically, then set down his glass. "Wait... what?"

The fae glanced down at his plate, looking uncharacteristically shy. "It was a Lithian heron. Leonor presented it to me this morning."

He and Dylan shared a quick glance. One that told Katerina there was a lot more cultural significance that she didn't understand. It was a fleeting moment, then Dylan flashed a casual grin.

"Aw, Cass... you've always wanted a bird."

The fae gave him a playful shove and turned back to Aidan, while Katerina tugged curiously on his sleeve to make him explain. He pulled their chairs closer together, leaning his head down with a smile, until a throat cleared sharply from across the room.

It was a quiet sound. One that only a shifter could have heard. But every muscle in Dylan's body stiffened at the same time as the smile melted off his face.

"It's, uh..." He took a giant swig of whiskey, trying hard to play it off. "The Lithian heron is one of those—"

"I overheard you and Atticus today," Katerina admitted softly.

Dylan's eyes flashed over with a start, but he was quick to compose himself. Even quicker to offer a careless smile. As if the words of his most trusted advisor couldn't matter less.

"Yes. I've been ordered to marry a girl from Belaria." His eyes flashed ever so quickly across the room before he offered his girlfriend another smile. "But don't worry, I have a plan."

"You have a plan," Katerina repeated blankly, well aware that, as a shifter, Atticus Gail was quite capable of overhearing every word. "Do tell."

Dylan downed the rest of his drink and poured himself another. "I plan to have them all killed."

Katerina spat out a mouthful of Champagne. Across the ballroom, Atticus rubbed his temples with a quiet sigh. "Excuse me?"

"Careful, love." Dylan dabbed her face with a napkin. "You're far too pretty to choke."

"You plan to kill all the women in Belaria?" she repeated, kicking him under the table.

"Mass execution." He leaned back with a little smirk, looking quite proud of himself for concocting such a clever plan. "No brides available. Problem solved."

At this point Atticus poured a stiff drink of his own, while Katerina fought back a smile.

"See, I can't make jokes like that. Because of my dad."

"Oh, Kat—that must be really hard for you," Aidan inserted, tuning back in. "What a heavy price to pay for all that bloodshed and death."

She spritzed him with some Champagne, and he flashed her a pearly smile.

"At any rate, you shouldn't antagonize your councilmen," Cassiel chided softly, giving Dylan a stern look. "We haven't put them in the easiest position."

Dylan's smile vanished as he reached for the bottle. "I couldn't care less about their position."

"You should—"

"It's not the same for you, Cass."

"It's not the *same*?" Cassiel repeated incredulously, intercepting the whiskey and putting it safely out of reach. "Dylan, my people were almost wiped out. Completely exterminated. All they talk about is repopulation." His eyes flickered over to his delegation as his shoulders tightened with an invisible weight. "I'm their prince, and my girl-friend's not exactly Fae."

The smile froze on Katerina's face as a chill ran up her spine. "What about your girlfriend?"

At that moment, the very girl in question peeled herself away from the crowd and wandered back to their table, plopping herself down in a vacant chair.

"Different girlfriend." Cassiel leaned back, draping an arm across her shoulders. A quick glance at the others warned them to be quiet. "Where have you been?"

Her face brightened dramatically. "Off diplomatting!"

"Oh yeah?" He looked amused. "Diplomatting?"

"And I'm bloody good at it!" she gushed. "I just got the Venkwje to agree to host the annual woodland joust in exchange for autumnal grazing rights." She kicked back in her chair, happily stealing his drink for herself. "Coincidentally, what is a yak?"

...*seriously*?

Cassiel shot her a panicked look and hurried to undo the damage, while Katerina glanced at Dylan with a hint of concern. She knew the man well enough to tell when he was evading. She just didn't know how serious a problem this marriage issue was going to be.

"Hon, all jokes aside, do you think we should talk about—"

"*Your Majesty.*"

The pair glanced up in surprise as a tall man in a travelling cloak came to stand before the table. He bowed low before glancing up at Ka-terina with a familiar smile.

"It's been a long time."

She pushed to her feet in surprise, staring him up and down. "Mat-ti?"

Dylan looked on silently as she darted around the edge of the table and met him in the middle of the floor, hurrying through the ceremonial logistics, before giving him a tight hug.

"I can't believe you're here!" she exclaimed. "I thought you were off somewhere in the Western Territories, fighting alongside your dad."

"Plans change." He brushed back his hair with a smile, looking windswept and handsome, as though he'd just leapt off a horse. "When I heard about the summit, I started heading back straight away. Would have gotten here a lot sooner, but there was some flooding—"

"What a shame, we might have missed you altogether."

The two of them glanced up to see Dylan regarding them with a steady smile. That kind that made him seem ironically threatening. The kind that never reached his eyes.

Katerina took a quick step back, suddenly finding herself in unfamiliar territory, then hurried to make the proper introductions. "Matti, this is Dylan Hale. King of Belaria. Ruler of the Northern Kingdom. High Sovereign of the Fifth Realm." She gestured from one to the next. "Dylan this is Sir Matthew Lansbury, son of—"

"I know who you are." Despite the steely smile, Dylan's voice was friendly enough. He, too, walked around the table and shook the man's hand. "Our fathers fought together in Esterworth."

Katerina froze as she had a sudden flashback. Clinging to the edge of a cliff in the middle of the wilderness. Dodging Dylan's prying questions about the suitors who'd attempted to court her in the past. Reeling in surprise when he recognized the name of Carl Lansbury's son.

"That's right, they did," Matthew replied, eyeing the king's casual posture, the way his arm slid around Katerina's waist. "Back before returning to Belaria."

...where the entire Hale family proceeded to die.

She wasn't sure whether it was intentional or not, but an icy chill fell over the reunion. The likes of which might have ended quite badly if Aidan hadn't picked that moment to join them.

"Kat, it's almost time for the speeches. Are you ready?" She nodded just as he noticed the stranger in their midst. "Oh, pardon me. Aidan Dorsett." He extended a hand. "Nice to meet you."

It was a pleasant enough introduction but Matthew froze perfectly still, looking as though he'd been struck with some kind of wide-eyed paralysis. Dylan's lips twitched up in a smirk, while Katerina was merely confused. Aidan's eyes cooled as he lowered the hand and walked away.

"*Matti*," Katerina hissed the second he was out of earshot, "what the heck was that?"

The frozen knight blinked, shuddered, then slowly came back to life. "I'm sorry... was that a vampire?"

At this point, Dylan chuckled and walked away—clearly deeming the rival unworthy of his time—while Katerina rolled her eyes and dismissed him. "Yeah, it was."

The ice sculptures had melted to the point of unrecognizability, and the last of the dessert trays had been cleared away. Katerina intercepted a pointed nod from Abel Bishop and pushed gracefully to her feet, clearing her throat as the room fell suddenly and respectfully silent.

"Greetings, friends, and welcome to this most historic event. A gathering of the leaders of the five kingdoms. The first step of a most sincere effort to create a lasting peace within the realm."

There was a polite spattering of applause. A scripted moment where all of said leaders discreetly eyed the people at the tables beside them. Measuring resistance. Calculating the odds.

"First of all, on behalf of the High Kingdom, I want to thank you all for coming." Katerina's eyes shone with sincerity as they rested upon each delegation in turn. "The road that brought us here has not been without its share of sacrifice and grief. I fully acknowledge the part my own family played, and you have my solemn vow that in the years to come we will make amends."

In a controversial vote amongst the friends several weeks before, it was decided that the queen should mention the elephant in the room straight away in the hopes of moving past it. It was a gesture they decided would be appreciated by some, and at the very least would demand some degree of respect. That was in theory. In practice, it was a bit more awkward than everyone had thought. There was a restless shifting throughout the crowd, and Kailas slid lower in his seat.

"Over the next few days, we hope to embark upon a path that will bring a lasting peace to all of our great peoples." Katerina's voice rang out with authority, holding the attention of everyone in the room. "To lay the foundations of a united future that will last for generations to come."

At this point, Tanya had recommended inserting a joke. The queen wisely chose to move on.

"I know this will not be easy. I know that expectations will be challenged and concessions will be made along the way. But if we can find it in ourselves to take a step back, to put aside those suppositions and see the bigger picture, I believe we can be more than what we are today."

Her voice rose like the tide, building momentum as the room hung on every word.

"I believe we can cast off those differences that separate us, and come to realize that we are stronger together than we are divided. That we can achieve more together than we could ever do on our own. And if we just trust one another, if we just take that single leap of faith, we can start to build ourselves a world where—"

There was a swish of air, followed by a piercing scream.

It took a moment for Katerina to realize what had happened. For her to gather her wits enough to realize that someone had shot off an arrow.

An arrow that had lodged itself in the wall beside her brother's head.

Chapter 6

There was a piercing scream, one that carried farther than Katerina's words ever could. A single ringing cry. Then the world began to crumble.

"Get down!"

Katerina's hands clamped over her mouth as a pair of strong arms caught her around the waist. Two chairs down, Kailas was frozen in shock—one hand drifting up to the gash on his cheek where the arrow had grazed his skin. People were shouting. A woman was screaming. A hundred chairs were flying backwards as the delegations sprang to their feet.

"Dylan, what—"

But her boyfriend had vanished. Only the warrior remained.

His body curved protectively over her own. Arms wrapping around every exposed inch of skin. Piercing eyes scanning the room as he tried to see where the arrow had come from. In times like this, she'd swear he couldn't even hear her. His only thought was to defend.

It wasn't the easiest task. Shoot an arrow into a room full of ancient blood feuds, and guess what you'll get? Chaos. Complete and utter chaos.

"Kailas!" Katerina turned to her brother instead, trying to see him through the tangle of bodies in between. "Kailas! Are you all right?!"

He was still sitting in exactly the same place. Staring out at the wreckage. Unaware that his face had started dripping blood.

She shouted for the guards to move him. He was an easy target as long as he remained. But, to her extreme surprise, it was Cassiel who grabbed him, throwing him roughly to the floor as his bright eyes made a tactical sweep of the room. He was yelling something at his little sister. Yelling at the top of his lungs, but Katerina was still unable to hear. A second later, she realized why.

While half of the tables had turned on each other—shouting and cursing and pulling out hidden weapons to ward off a possible attack—the other half was stampeding across the ballroom.

Straight towards the seven friends seated on the other side.

"Your Majesty!"

Katerina looked up just as a swarm of guards barreled straight through center of the long banquet table. Weapons raised and ready. Eyes locked on their target. Leaving a sea of shattered porcelain in their wake. She and Dylan were ripped apart before either one could realize what was happening. Vanished from sight inside a protective circle of men.

The rest of the friends were having a similar experience.

Tanya picked up a carving knife and leapt up onto the table, prepared to take down the sniper, only to be immediately taken down herself. A wave of witches, dryads, and other supernatural transplants pulled her instantly out of the line of fire—lifting her clean off her feet as they carried her away. Aidan had no representatives there besides himself, but Dylan appeared to have left specific instructions for his own men if negotiations went south. The second their king was secure the Belarian guards leapt forward and grabbed the vampire as well, forgetting their instinctual fear as they surrounded him in a protective arch, an impenetrable fortress of blades.

Cassiel had no better luck.

No sooner had he drawn his sword and rushed forward, then a line of Fae warriors sprang up in his path. He froze where he stood, staring at them in surprise, before they swept forward and seized him by the arms, dragging him backwards out of the fray.

And then there were none.

Kailas and Serafina were being held together, and Tanya and Aidan had disappeared from view. Cassiel glanced impatiently over the heads of his captors, still searching for the person who had fired, but allowed himself to be led away. The ranger was not so compliant.

"Let me *go!*"

Katerina swiveled around, staring between the gaps in her own people as Dylan thrashed and strained against his guards. Despite the valiant effort, he was making little headway. It was thirty to one, and no sooner had he thrown off the people holding him, than ten more took their place.

"Atticus!"

It was only then that Katerina saw the giant wolf. Teeth bared. Claws extended. Promising a swift and grisly death to anyone who dared approach his king.

"I know you can hear me!" Dylan shouted again, even more furious that his violent protests were being ignored. "Atticus! I *command* you to release me!"

The wolf turned around slowly, and even Katerina could see the sarcasm in his eyes.

Really? You think that's going to work?

A petulant scowl flitted across the king's face as he pushed up the crown to keep it from tipping into his eyes. "What's the point of even having this thing, if you guys don't—"

"Filthy beasts!"

A loud voice cut through the clamor, and the friends turned around to see a fae and a dwarf squaring off in the middle of the room. They were soon joined by others. And more after that.

"The arrow came from the southwest corner," the fae continued, his bright eyes sparking with hatred and rage. "Only one group was sitting there."

He was instantly backed by three of his countrymen, but the dwarves had numbers of their own. And they didn't take kindly to the accusation.

"An arrow, was it?" The dwarf-lord standing before him may have only come up to his chest, but he packed quite a punch as he slammed a battle-axe into the floor. "Does it look like we fight with bows and arrows? Sounds more like Fae to me! Isn't archery your specialty?"

The fae let out a fierce profanity, his hand curling around the grip of a knife.

"And when have you ever known a fae to miss?"

"Why does it matter to you, anyway?" A witch stepped between them, pink and violet sparks shooting from her hands. "There isn't a person in the five kingdoms who doesn't want Kailas dead."

"I care not for the Damaris boy," the fae snarled, keeping his eyes on the dwarf, "but the arrow could have struck my own prince!"

"We all had people sitting at that table," a shifter from Belaria growled. "And frankly, it's the Kreo who have the most to lose." He spat on the floor. "A tribe of people with a *shape-shifter* as their queen. It's disgraceful."

The witch hit him with a ball of glowing light. There was a violent uproar from the rest of the crowd. But the fae and his companions merely rolled their eyes.

"Shape-shifters. Wolves. There is no difference. Just a few short decades on this earth, then you return to dust where everyone looks the same. You are not here long enough to matter."

The shifter growled, his fingers elongating into frightening claws. "Funny, I didn't think there were enough of your people left to make that claim—"

That did it.

The rest of the crowd exploded in on itself. Dissolving in a chaotic tangle of swearing and blades. Shifters versus Fae. Goblins versus men. Witches versus whoever happened to be standing too close. A sea of embroidered cloaks and ball gowns, all tearing at the seams.

Katerina went very still. Watching the scene in front of her with wide eyes. She considered ways she could stop it. She considered things she might say. But everything fell short.

The delegations hadn't come for dinner. They'd come expecting something like this.

A weary sigh shuddered through her body, and she glanced around to see her friends watching as well. All with identical expressions. All with the same hopeless look in their eyes.

One thing's for sure... our peace summit is off to a fantastic start.

THE BANQUET GOT CANCELLED. The delegations were sent to separate wings of the castle. The servants were tasked with mopping the blood off the ballroom floor.

Katerina and her gang of misfits were whisked away to a 'safe room', where no fewer than five doctors proceeded to needlessly examine them for injuries. Rather, no fewer than five doctors tried.

The gang turned out to be less than receptive.

"For heaven's sake, Your Majesty." Atticus pressed his fingers together in a desperate sort of prayer. "Will you please just shift back?"

A chocolate brown wolf stared back at him. Sitting defiantly on a pile of discarded clothes.

"Ambassador, if you would just—"

An already hesitant doctor froze as Aidan slowly turned around to meet his gaze. The vampire hadn't taken kindly to being manhandled by the Belarian soldiers even if their intentions had been good. A checkup by the royal physician proved to be one push too far.

"How quaint." His voice blistered with sarcasm as he eyed the medical equipment clutched in the man's hand. "Tell me, Doctor, do you have the faintest idea *what I am?*"

"Maybe's he's volunteering," Tanya said with a smirk. "Only one way to heal a vampire."

As the doctor turned his fearful eyes her way, she shifted into him with a spiteful *pop*. He let out a startled gasp, then dropped his equipment and rushed from the room.

"You are acting like a *child*," Atticus hissed, lowering his voice so as to not be heard by the others.

The wolf stood up on its back legs, methodically knocking all the portraits off the wall.

"Manners, Dylan. Some of those paintings are older than me." Cassiel alternated between chiding his friend and threatening the doctor. "*I unequivocally refuse treatment. Be gone from my sight.* On second thought, they all were commissioned by Thaddeus the Fourth—feel free to tear them up a little. *Touch me, and that hand will never touch anything again.*"

"My lord, will you please allow me to—", one doctor begged of Kailas.

"No."

It was a one-word answer, but it was enough. The citizens of the free world had long ago learned not to question Kailas Damaris once he'd made up his mind.

...all except his girlfriend.

"Sit still," she commanded, taking the gauze from the doctor and gently dabbing the cut beneath his eye. "This is going to need a stitch. Wait there while I get some thread."

Round and round it went. Everyone resisting, or refusing, or imploring, or generally doing their best not to get bitten by the wolf. Only Katerina was sitting still. Her eyes locked on her brother. A look of cold fury whitening the edges of her face.

"I'm sorry!" Atticus finally conceded. "I'm sorry to have restrained you back at the banquet! I'm sorry for commanding the guards to take you away! There—will that suffice?!"

The wolf stared at him for a moment, then a handsome man appeared in its place. "For now."

The councilman looked to the heavens for strength, then took off his cloak and draped it over the arms of his sovereign. The rest of the doctors had been sufficiently frightened away, and by the time Dylan took a seat beside his girlfriend the entire group was ready for some answers.

"What happened?" Aidan demanded, staring at each of the various representatives in turn. "I refuse to believe that someone pulled out a bow and fired off a shot without anyone seeing."

Under any other circumstances, he would have had a point. But whoever had attempted to take the prince's life had planned it perfectly. Firing off the shot the one moment that no one would be looking. The one moment when everyone would be watching the queen give her speech.

Even Dylan's sharp eyes didn't see where it had come from.

"Bad timing, huh?" Tanya muttered in an undertone to Katerina. "Told you there should have been a joke..."

The queen ignored her, still staring fixedly at her brother. He was in the process of getting his face stitched by Serafina. Hardly blinking an eye as the needle dipped into his skin.

"Someone had to have seen something," Cassiel murmured, throwing a quick glance at his sister before turning back to his own men. "We'll break them up into groups, find out—"

"My brother and I need the room."

Katerina didn't phrase it as a question. Nor did she break her piercing gaze. As the others turned in surprise she kept her eyes locked on Kailas. Looking a breath away from murder herself.

"Are you okay?" Dylan asked quietly, glancing warily between the siblings. He hadn't been pleased when they'd found themselves alone at the beginning of the evening. He wasn't eager to repeat the incident now. "Would you like me to..." He trailed off, seeing the look on her face.

He nodded quickly at the others and they filed out the door. Each brimming with silent questions. Each fighting the urge to stay. Serafina was the last to go, and she did so with great reluctance. Casting each a worried look as she swept away.

Kailas waited until the door closed before turning to his sister. There was a question in his eyes, and a tiny piece of thread was still dangling from his cheek. He caught her looking, was just about to take it out himself, when she stormed across the room and slapped him right in the face.

Hard.

"Katy, what—"

She hit him again. Even harder this time.

"Katerina," he gasped, "what are you—"

A third strike.

"What the heck's going on?!"

Before she could hit him again he leapt to his feet, staring down at her in shock. Never once, not in eighteen years, had he seen her be violent. That was always his role. Hers was to watch silently from the sidelines. Not counting the time she'd set their childhood mentor on fire.

Katerina couldn't even answer. She just raised her hand again.

"*Enough*!" He caught her wrist an inch away from his face, holding it accusingly in the air between them. "What's the matter with you?!"

There was a momentary pause, a suspended moment, where brother and sister looked at each other with bated breath, then all hell broke loose.

"ME?!" A wave of liquid fire poured out of Katerina's hands, setting the examination table on fire. "What's the matter with YOU?!"

The prince's mouth fell open with genuine bewilderment, and he shook his head. "Katerina, I don't know what—"

"YOU JUST SAT THERE!"

A deathly quiet fell over the room as both siblings froze perfectly still. One was looking like she could set the five kingdoms on fire. The other was looking like he'd been caught in a lie.

"I've seen you move, Kailas. I've seen you fight." Katerina's eyes flashed as her voice grew dangerously quiet. "You've dodged faster arrows than that before."

His face paled and it was suddenly easy to see the bruises from sleeplessness beneath his eyes. The perpetual shadows that no amount of sleep or sunlight could seem to erase. "I didn't..." He cleared his throat and tried again. "I didn't see it coming."

"Yes, you did." She was in no mood to be lied to, and he was in no position to deny it. One way or another, the truth was coming out. "You saw it coming and you just *sat* there."

He looked ready to deny it. He looked ready to close the book on the whole night and storm from the room. But the longer he stood there, the more that faded. The longer he stood there the more that arrogant, defensive man disappeared, leaving a heartbroken teenager standing in his wake. "Why would I have moved?"

The question caught her completely off guard. Melted that anger clean out of her as she stared at her brother with a horrible kind of shock.

"Why would you have..." She trailed off, unable to repeat the question. "We're going to find out who did it, Kailas. I swear, we're going to find out—"

"It doesn't matter who did it." A quiet devastation tore through him, and he suddenly looked years beyond his age. "It doesn't matter who specifically fired the shot. Everyone in the five kingdoms wants me dead. And why wouldn't they? The things that I've..." A violent shudder shook his entire body, leaving him completely bereft in its wake. "I don't deserve to be here, Katy. I don't deserve to live."

It took the queen a moment to realize her cheeks were wet. Another moment after that to realize she was crying. She had vowed long ago to never cry over Kailas. She'd done it too many times before. Lost everything that part of herself had to give.

But the man sitting in front of her wasn't the boy she used to know.

The one whose mischievous smile had sharpened into a callous grin. The one who'd lost that sparkling effervescence. The irresistible charm that had left her breathless with laughter as a child.

...and now he wants to die.

It seemed as though there was nothing left to say. What did you tell a man who'd decided he no longer wanted to live? What words could possibly make a difference?

"No."

A faint crease appeared on the prince's forehead as he stared at her with wide, haunted eyes.

"No?" he repeated softly. "What does that—"

"You don't get to do that to me." Each word was slow and precise, levelled at him with quiet determination. "You killed our father. Divided our land. Chased me out of the kingdom and left me in the wilderness to die." Their eyes locked. "You don't get to take away my brother, too."

More than anything else that had happened, *this* seemed to make an impression.

His body flinched, as if he was feeling that arrow for the first time, and his eyes shone with a kind of sadness his sister would never understand.

"You think I don't think about that every day?" His voice dropped to a rough whisper. "The way he looked up at me? The way it felt? Every time I walk past his room..."

A wave of emotion bowed his head, and suddenly the queen wasn't the only one crying.

"I want it to be over. I can't... I just want it all to stop."

The words unlocked a painful memory, echoing back in another man's voice. A man ripped to pieces by sins that had been beyond his control. A fourteen-year-old boy, standing on a ledge.

...I just wanted it to stop.

It was like a veil fell away. The last eight years of bloodshed and terror momentarily lifted, and the queen was able to see her twin brother standing underneath.

Bruised, broken, but not beyond repair. Not beyond redemption.

"Well, this isn't just about you." Katerina straightened up to her full height, suddenly sure of her course. Suddenly sure what the *next* few words should be. "You are my family, Kailas. The *only* family I have left. You don't get to feel sorry for yourself. You don't get to act like there aren't people out there who still love you... because there *are* people out there who still love you."

For a fleeting moment, she took his hand. Then she swept briskly to the door.

"You are my *brother*. Start acting like it."

It was quite possibly the strangest reconciliation the five kingdoms had ever seen. It was certainly the most unexpected. Kailas had frozen dead still when she'd touched him, staring down like he could still see her hand. He looked up with a start when she cleared her throat, cocking her head towards the safe room door.

"You coming?"

He hesitated a moment, then peeled himself swiftly off the wall. Straightening his clothes and smoothing down his hair as he joined his sister by the door. "I'm coming." A hint of humor flashed through his eyes. The faintest flicker of a smile she hadn't seen in many years. "Anything else?"

She glanced down at the doorknob, hair spilling forward to hide a smile of her own. "Yeah, take that needle out of your face. It's disgusting."

The door pulled open and the rest of the friends stumbled backwards into the hall. Not even attempting to hide the fact that they'd been eavesdropping. There were averted eyes and awkward glances, but before anyone could speak a windswept messenger came tearing down the hall. Pale face. Frightened eyes. And a streak of what looked like blood on the back of his hands.

"Your Majesty..." He skidded to a stop in front of Katerina, shaking head to toe as he sank into a deep bow. "...we have a problem."

Chapter 7

We found something in the woods.
        Never good words.

Ever.

Didn't matter the timing. Didn't matter the context. There are some words, when strung together, that are never good to hear.

Katerina marched purposefully into the forest. A torch in her hand. A pair of high heels dangling from her hand. There was no longer any cause for pretense. No need to play dress up and stand on ceremony. That ship had sailed when an assassin's arrow drew the blood of the crown prince. Her brother.

All that was left now was damage control. Contain the situation. Find the person responsible. And deal with whatever mess was out in the woods. And quickly.

They were already holding the peace summit together with their bare hands.

"You say he wouldn't tell you what it was?" the queen asked in a low murmur. Dylan was walking tall by her side, but it was to Hastings the guard she directed the question.

"No, milady," he replied, hand ready on the grip of his blade. "Only that it was not dangerous to your person."

Dylan glanced quickly to the side before returning his gaze to the trees. "Not dangerous to your person, but the man looked like he was about to faint. There's danger in it somewhere."

Even though he was right, Katerina felt no fear. Perhaps it was the people standing beside her. A Fae warrior, a vampire, a shape-shifter, a king. Perhaps it was the fact that she had already set these woods aflame and could do so again at a moment's notice. Perhaps she was simply grateful to be doing something that made her feel alive.

But for the first time since she'd returned to the castle, the queen didn't notice the infernal weight of her crown. She felt only the warm glow of her mother's amulet pulsing against her skin.

Of course, all that changed dramatically when they came to a clearing in the trees.

The entire party instinctively stopped. Over sixty guards and delegates, standing en masse behind their young sovereigns. Katerina squinted at the crumpled form in the grass, but it was bathed in shadow and hard to see. Instead, she reached out to a tall man standing by her side.

"Aidan?"

The vampire didn't need his superior senses to answer her question. Nor did he need his ability to see in the dark.

He simply listened for a moment, then shook his head. "There's no pulse."

Again, it should have been comforting. With how many people had tried to kill them in the last few months, no pulse was one less thing to worry about. But it had the opposite effect. Instead, the queen was filled with a sense of dread as she crossed the clearing and stared down into the grass.

It was the dwarf from the banquet hall. The one who'd slammed down his battle-axe and gone head to head with the fae. One of the prime instigators of the night's commotion.

Now lying face-down in the dirt.

"How did he get all the way out here?" she asked quietly, gazing around. They were almost half a league from the castle. And the castle had been on lock-down since the assassination attempt.

Abel Bishop shifted uneasily as the dwarf chieftain pushed his way through the crowd.

"After you and your companions were escorted to safety, I gave permission for each of the kingdoms to send representatives into the woods. To search for the assassin. Most of them have already returned. I guess... this one didn't."

Dylan clenched his jaw and gave Atticus a pointed glare. Clearly he disagreed. Had he not been 'escorted to safety,' he would have led such a search himself. And most likely apprehended the assailant.

The councilman bowed his head as the ranger dropped to his knees. Not quite touching the body, but examining it nonetheless. Working with impossibly gentle hands.

"There was a struggle, but I can't tell what killed him," he murmured, running his fingers over the ground by the dwarf's side. "There's no wound. No sign of—"

"And why the hell are you just *guessing*?!" a gruff voice interrupted.

Katerina looked up with a start as a burly dwarf burst into the clearing. He was shaped like a barrel, heavily muscled, with stout arms and legs, and a crown of rusted bronze was holding back his grizzled black hair. One look at his fallen countryman, and his eyes darkened with rage.

"Why guess," he barked again, "when you can just ask *this* one what happened?"

Katerina turned in surprise as he pointed to the band of fae standing on the periphery of the crowd. They were staring at the corpse just like everyone else, but seemed to have no better idea what had happened than anyone else. The dwarf leveled his finger at one fae in particular; the tall dark-haired warrior who had argued with the slain dwarf in the middle of the hall.

Oh crap, this is not going to end well.

The fae looked up in genuine surprise. Flickers of torchlight dancing across his pale skin. "I didn't." An uneasy murmur went through the crowd behind him, and his bright eyes flew straight to Cassiel. "My lord, I swear it—"

"He lies!" the dwarf-lord shouted.

Behind him, the crowd was getting riled. Those who believed the fae, siding against those who didn't. All still heavily armed in the darkness. All still well aware of the body in their midst.

"My lord," the fae only had eyes for Cassiel, "I never touched the dwarf. You have my word."

Truth be told, the handsome warrior looked far less concerned with the fact that he was being accused of murder than he was with the possibility of disappointing his prince. His eyes swept over the fallen dwarf without much regard one way or another, focused only on his own kin. It was insensitive, to be sure. Aloof to the point of callousness. But the one thing he didn't look was guilty.

Katerina's instinct was to believe him.

"My lord?"

Cassiel glanced at the man for only a moment. Only a moment, but it was enough.

"I know," he murmured, so quietly that no one could hear.

But in this case, just knowing would not be enough. The dwarves were out for blood. The rest of the summit was already beginning to turn on each other. And the word of one fae would not suffice to pardon another. They needed someone impartial. A third-party judge.

Dylan and Cassiel's friendship was well-known. The people were unlikely to trust a vampire, or place much credence in the verdict of the Kreo. That meant there was just one kingdom left.

"I will speak to him," Katerina declared, her voice ringing out in the darkness as a sudden hush fell over the rest of the woods. "I will speak to him and discover the truth."

Only she was close enough to catch Cassiel's secret look of gratitude. To everyone else, he kept his eyes fixed thoughtfully on the body, glancing up only to give her a permissive nod.

"As for everyone else, I suggest you return to the castle and get some rest."

She watched with wide, worried eyes as the lifeless dwarf was lifted from the ground, carried away on the shoulders of his countrymen.

"We have a long day of peace talks ahead of us." No one responded to her words. It was as if the word 'peace' no longer existed among them. She wondered momentarily if things were better now or when her father reigned. She pushed the thought away and strode hesitantly forward. It was time to work. Not time to ponder.

ALL KATERINA WANTED after the day she'd had was to crawl into her bed, use her boyfriend's body as a warm blanket, and fall into a dreamless sleep. Whether it was the assassination attempt, the impromptu reconciliation with her brother, or the late-night homicide in the woods—she was utterly spent.

The one thing she did *not* want to do was interrogate a Fae warrior in the dungeons by herself. A man who was most likely innocent, and was probably fifty times her age.

"Thank you for agreeing to speak with me." She gestured awkwardly to the chairs that had been set up in the middle of the empty hall. The same hall that had been recently rebuilt after her brother had shifted into a dragon and burst through the walls. "I know it's very late—"

"I am here because my lord commands it," the fae answered shortly. But he did consent to sit, glancing briefly around the dungeon in the process. "I see you've renovated."

What a dick.

You didn't like how it was before?" she quipped wearily.

He turned back to the queen, lips curving up in a humorless smile. "Not after having spent time here myself."

Ding, ding, ding—round one to the fae.

Katerina glanced up in alarm, then straightened quickly. Trying her best not to imagine the circumstances under which such an imprisonment had happened. Or how he had possibly escaped.

Just calm down, she told herself. *You outrank this guy. You're best friends with his beloved leader. Just ask him some questions, and be done. Cassiel is waiting right upstairs.*

"I did not lay a hand on the dwarf," the fae declared preemptively. He definitely wasn't cordial about it, but there was no deception on his lovely face. "Not since the banquet. Where he went after that and what happened to him is a mystery to me."

Katerina stifled a sigh. She believed him. Without a doubt. But there was protocol to be followed, and she couldn't help but chafe at the unfeeling way he'd spoken.

"Not that you really care, right?" She couldn't help but ask the question, nor could she keep the sharp edge from her voice. "Back in the ballroom you called the lot of them 'filthy beasts.'"

Most people would have been intimidated to find themselves on the wrong end of a murder interrogation with an irritable queen. Most people would have been intimidated to find themselves in the dungeon at all. The fae only smiled. A beautiful, terrible smile that didn't reach his eyes.

"I am not here because of my opinion of the little man. I'm here because he's dead. A misfortune I had no part of. The way I felt about the man is no crime."

The fae should have stopped there. He should have left it at that. But the indignity of being interrogated by a mortal in a Damaris dungeon had clearly left him unable to resist.

"I would not be here *at all* were it not for the express wish of my prince."

Flippin' straight. The express wish of your prince.

"That's right." Katerina regained her footing with a spiteful smile. "Cass ordered you to come down here and speak with me." She deliberately used the nickname and watched with great satisfaction the effect it had on the fae. "And as someone who knows him very well, I can assure you he won't be at all pleased with your cavalier attitude. Nor will he be at all pleased with the manner in which you are speaking to one of his closest friends, a queen."

Like dousing a candle, all the anger and spite rushed out of the fae. Rather, it cooled to a low simmer, carefully contained in his eyes. With what looked like the greatest effort, he bowed his head and softened his voice to a more respectful tone. "Forgive me, Your Majesty. It has been a long night."

It *had* been a long night. Preceded by a *very* long day. And although she knew better, that this frustrated man was innocent and being lectured to by a child, she found herself unable to resist.

"The fate of every man, woman, and child in the five kingdoms rests upon the success of this peace summit," she chided punishingly. "This is a time for renewed understanding and compromise, not the resurrection of ancient prejudice and feuds."

A very peculiar expression came over the fae's face and he pushed to his feet. Pacing slowly back and forth, he periodically flexed his hands.

"If you and the others can't set aside your differences in the banquet hall, then what example does that set for the rest of the people?" she continued. "How do we proceed to implement widespread changes throughout the land?"

He nodded distractedly at what she was saying, but his mind was clearly on other things. A faint sheen of sweat had appeared on his forehead, and there was an unnatural dilation to his pupils.

"At any rate," she pushed to her feet with a sigh, "there would never have been a way to prove your guilt one way or another. I hereby clear you of all charges—"

There was a broken gasp as the fae collapsed where he stood. Dark hair spilling over the floor of the dungeon. Cringing against the stone in unimaginable pain.

"Kerien!" Katerina exclaimed, repeating a name she'd heard Cassiel use as she dropped to her knees beside him. "What—"

"Thasos illumine." He convulsed on the floor, fighting for breath. "I can't..."

With a soft cry, he flipped onto his back. Silent tears streaming down his face. A look of sheer terror in his eyes as he gazed up into the darkness above. It was then Katerina saw it, the glassy sheen that had settled over those bright, eternal eyes. Her face paled in horror and she covered her mouth.

The fae was blind.

"Caros!"

She recognized the Fae word for 'help' and sprang back to life. Propping him up uselessly in her lap. Laying a cool hand on his burning brow. Trying her best to ease whatever pain she could.

"I'm here," she whispered, too frightened to give it any strength. "What can I do?"

He turned at the sound of her voice and caught the tip of her hand, holding on tightly as he gazed into the abyss. She held on with equal strength. Stroking his hair. Whispering useless nothings. Weeping with silent tears as a fearless immortal fell apart in her arms.

A final tremor shook through him. For a breathless moment, his body went completely still.

He lifted his head slightly and whispered, "Taviel..."

Then he lay down his head and died.

Katerina stared at the fae for a full minute. Frozen with shock. Breathless with fear. Unable to look away from the sudden tranquility that had settled over his lifeless eyes.

Then she let out a terrified scream.

There was a bang from somewhere outside the dungeon. The sound of sprinting footsteps flying down the stone hall. The door burst open just a second later, flooding the garish scene with torchlight. Illuminating the queen and the fae in the center of the room.

Cassiel froze perfectly still. A breathless portrait of fear and surprise. His lips parted for a moment as the nightmare washed over him. Then he heard the queen sob.

"He's dead."

In a flash, he was kneeling by her side. Grabbing the fae away from her as she stumbled to her feet. Reeling in horror as he stared down at the man's sightless eyes.

"Kerien," he gasped, shaking him. "Kerien, please!"

It was no use. It had been clear from the moment he stepped inside that the fae was beyond saving. The prince murmured something in his native tongue, then let out a fierce cry.

"What the heck happened!" Silent tears poured down his face, catching in his long blond hair. "You were just supposed to *talk* to him—"

"I did!" Katerina cried. "Cass, I swear to you, I don't know what happened! One second we were just talking, and the next—"

"Kat!"

A second later, Dylan was there. He had been loitering just a few floors up, waiting for the interrogation to be over, and came running the second he heard raised voices.

His face went dangerously pale when he saw the lifeless fae. That same blindsiding shock swept over him, freezing him momentarily in his tracks, before he sprang into action once more.

"Cass! Don't touch him!" he yelled, kicking away the fae's hands with enough strength to break bone. "We don't know what happened; maybe it's a curse!"

The man who didn't believe in curses had been recently convinced. And the sight of two bodies, discovered just hours apart, was enough to throw him into a mild panic.

"Cassiel, *please!*" he repeated, as the fae clung onto the body. "It isn't safe!"

"He couldn't see..." Katerina mumbled, wrapping her arms around her chest. "One second we were just talking to each other, and the next... he couldn't see."

Cassiel was crying. Katerina shaking. Dylan torn indecisively between the two. If it hadn't been for those next words, they might have stood there forever.

Katerina shivered and looked at Cass. "What is Taviel?"

A sudden hush descended on the room. Cassiel lifted his head. Dylan looked at her in amazement. For a second, everything was still. Then she found herself dangling in the air.

"Where did you hear that?" Cassiel didn't seem aware that he had lifted her off the ground, any more so than when he started crushing her against the wall. "Answer me, Katerina! Where did you hear that name!"

"Cass—"

Dylan placed a hand on his arm, but the fae was not to be moved. He held the queen there in a sort of daze. Staring deep into her eyes. Waiting breathlessly for an answer.

"It was Kerien," she gasped, feeling the fabric of her gown rip as her shoulder blades dug into the wall. "Right before he died... it was the only thing he said. Just one word. Taviel."

She was almost afraid to say it again. It spoke volumes to the fae's state of mine that Dylan hadn't made more of an effort to separate them. Instead, he was regarding his friend with a look of great caution. Like he'd given something very precious to a man who didn't know his own strength.

"What does it mean?" she whispered, wrapping her hands tentatively around his wrists. "Is it a name, or—"

Without any warning, she dropped to the ground. Landing with a twist of her ankle. Staring in muted shock as the fae swept away from her in the dark and vanished back up the stairs.

She and Dylan stared after him in silence.

His shoulders fell with a tired sigh.

"It's not a name. It's a place," he said quietly. "Taviel is the place where Cassiel grew up."

Chapter 8

Taviel was one of the oldest and most beautiful cities in the time of the Fae.

A shining capital of the ancient world. Built in the heart of three waterfalls in the middle of the evergreen forest for which it was named, the city was known far and wide for its majesty and splendor. People would travel for weeks just to seek counsel from its scholars. To gaze upon its ethereal beauty. To sit on the banks of the river and listen to its people rise up in song.

It was a city lost to legend and forgotten over time. Remembered now only by the dwindling immortals who remained. The sole keepers of its magic and secrets.

It was also, apparently, where Cassiel and Serafina grew up.

"Why don't they lead with stuff like that?" Katerina asked for the twelfth time, leaning back against the headboard of her massive canopy bed. "Hi, we're Serafina and Cassiel. We come from a mystical land of wonder and enchantment."

It was a question with no genuine answer, but Dylan chuckled softly and tried to answer it all the same. "They're Fae. Children of the stars. Their whole premise is wonder and enchantment."

Katerina sighed and tossed the remains of a candied fig onto the bed. "Yeah, I guess."

The castle had been placed on quarantine. Nobody allowed in or out. A claustrophobic decree, but no one was fighting it. Truth be told, after the inexplicable death of a Fae warrior and a dwarf battle-lord, nobody seemed to be in a particular hurry to be out on their own.

Left with no earthly explanation as to what had happened, an *unearthly* assumption was made.

It was decided that a witch must have put a curse on both parties. As Cassiel put it, 'Only the devil's magic could steal a man's sight.' Suspicion was resting heavily on the same witch who'd been arguing with both men earlier, but as no proof had been found any concrete accusations were still firmly stuck in the hypothetical. The witches vehemently denied it. A messenger was sent for Petra so she could come and 'sort it all out.'

Katerina had no idea what this meant, but Aidan assured her it would suffice.

So there she sat. Nestled under the arm of her boyfriend. Stress-eating candied figs. Damp hair from her bath dripping onto the silken sheets. The sugar and bath were supposed to calm her, but if anything they'd had the opposite effect. She'd had too much time on her own to sit and think of questions. Questions she was lobbing at her boyfriend at a relentless pace.

"So when you guys met, Cassiel never mentioned it?"

Dylan sighed, pushing back his hair. He'd been the one who'd pushed for the bath in the first place. It was a decision he seemed to be coming to regret.

"Not specifically. Not for a while, at least. I knew he was from some woodland realm; I knew he'd been a prince there. But every major stronghold of the Fae was completely demolished in the fight against your father. If he didn't want to talk about it, I didn't bring it up."

"But he did. I mean—*eventually*."

"Yeah." Dylan's lips twitched with an exasperated smile. "*Eventually*."

Katerina nodded to herself, completely oblivious to the effect she was having. It wasn't the first time she'd been around death. In the last few months, she'd seen it more times than she cared to remember. But it was the first time that someone had died in her arms. It was the first time she'd actually *felt* it. The precise moment when a person closed their eyes and ceased to be.

That's when she got out the figs. And started up with the questions. In hindsight, she may have been compartmentalizing just a bit.

"What's the story with the bird?"

At this point Dylan actually leaned forward, taking his arm from her shoulders and rubbing his face with a sigh. "Okay, did a bird just land on the window or something—"

"*Cassiel's* bird," she clarified, pelting him with a fig. "The one that attacked Aidan and weighs roughly the same as me."

"It attacked Aidan?" Dylan glanced back with a smile. "That's strangely poetic."

"Why?" she asked, grinning in spite of herself. "What does it mean?"

"It's a Lithian heron," he said simply, as if that explained everything. "The symbolic token of the Fae. Think of it as their spirit animal. There's nothing more sacred. Not on this earth."

Katerina scooted forward, draping his arm over herself once more. "Why? Why a heron?"

"It was the first thing that landed on the water when the great lords of the Fae defeated the giants and dark monsters of the Dunes. The first creature to come back and settle in a land that had been stripped bare." He spoke gently, reciting a story he'd heard as a child. "They took it as a sign. A return of hope. Built the foundations of their first city in that very spot."

Katerina stared at him, an automatic smile warming her face. Hearing it in his words, she could almost imagine. Just one tiny detail didn't seem to fit.

"Wait... *in that very spot*? Didn't you say the bird landed on the water?"

"Taviel was built at the junction of three waterfalls. A holy number. More symbolism." He waved a dismissive hand. "They're big on symbolism."

"Yeah, I'm starting to see that."

She recalled the look on Leonor's face when he'd presented the heron. She recalled the look on Cassiel's when he'd accepted it. It might have been a simple ceremony, over before it had even begun, but thinking through the anthologies of men she could find no equivalent.

"And they gave it to Cass," she murmured.

"Yeah," Dylan was abruptly thoughtful, staring out the window into the starry night, "they gave it to Cass. The next great hope of his people."

Katerina's smile faded as she remembered how the fae had looked in the dungeon, clinging to his fallen friend. Hope had been the last thing on his mind.

"Why would Kerien have said it?" she asked quietly, having an unexpectedly tough time saying the man's name. "Taviel. Why would that have been his last word?"

Dylan opened his mouth to answer, then glanced abruptly towards the door. "I think we're about to find out."

The door pushed open without a knock and the remaining five friends slipped inside. No one said much in terms of greeting but, after everything they'd shared over the last few months, one wasn't required. Instead, they merely settled themselves wearily on the bed. Casually intertwined.

Minutes passed. Minutes of tired, overwhelmed silence. Of quiet companionship and the small comfort of merely being close. Then Tanya glanced around with a crooked smile.

"You know, this is exactly what everyone says about us. That we're all sleeping together."

And THAT is why the world needs more shape-shifters.

Dylan let out a bark of laughter and Aidan bowed his head with a grin. There was a crack in the tension, and one by one everyone started coming out of it in their own way. Even Cassiel, who'd spent the last three hours threatening to decapitate a coven of witches, managed a small grin.

He gave his girlfriend's hand a squeeze, then sank onto the mattress beside Katerina, leaning his head back with a tired sigh. In a way, it was the most unguarded she'd ever seen him. Beating out even those moments when he'd been injured on the battlefield or fast asleep. There was a profound weariness in the way he was carrying himself. An endless exhaustion that seeped into his very bones.

"Well, it's official. They're closing the investigation and letting the witches go free."

"What?" Dylan sat up with a start, ready to fight or argue or scream if it would help to cheer up his friend. "How are they justifying that?! I can send for Atticus and—"

"It's fine." Cassiel held up a quieting hand. "It's done. They're leaving the rest to Petra."

"That's a wise choice," Aidan inserted quietly. "I know it's difficult now, but it will be better for everyone in the end. Trust me."

Katerina cast him a curious look, then turned to Cassiel instead. Not long before he'd pinned her against the wall of a dungeon, demanding answers for his fallen friend. Now, all that fight had gone out of him. He was a man in recovery. One of her dearest friends.

He felt her watching and slowly opened his eyes. A second later, he scooped her legs off the floor and was gently massaging her ankle. The same ankle she'd twisted when she fell.

I know you're sorry. I'm sorry, too.

If the others found this behavior at all strange, they didn't say so. Neither did they make any mention of the way Kailas was leaning casually against the wall behind his sister, absentmindedly twirling a lock of her fiery red hair.

"Peace talks are to resume tomorrow," Tanya said quietly.

"What?" This time it was Katerina who sat up with a start. "You've got to be kidding me."

"It's the reason we're all here," Serafina replied softly. "To find a way to make peace. It's the reason two people have already lost their lives."

Dylan's brow creased with a troubled frown. "We don't know the reason for that yet."

Cassiel pushed suddenly to his feet, unwilling to stay and talk about it a moment longer. "I'm going to send word to Kerien's family." He swept out the door without a backwards glance, speaking so quietly the others almost didn't hear the rest. "Whoever's left..."

Katerina watched him go with wide, worried eyes before turning to his sister. "Why did Kerien say it? Taviel?"

A look of that same ancient sadness clouded the fae's sparkling eyes. "That's where we grew up—his family, and ours. In their final moments, it's said people often think of home."

The queen absorbed this for a moment before venturing just one question more. "Then why did Cassiel freak out when he heard it?"

This time, no one stepped up to answer. There was a series of hastily averted looks and Serafina bowed her head. Finally, a full minute later, Dylan leaned forward with a sigh.

"Because his friend was lying dead at your feet. Because you're still a Damaris. And because your family set that entire city ablaze. Killed everyone who lived inside it. Had giants destroy the foundations so it could never be rebuilt."

That immortal beacon... turned to ashes and dust.

"Taviel became more than just the name of a city," Serafina continued softly. "The word began to mean something far greater. The death of every fae."

"They never speak it," Aidan added quietly. "I've never heard it said aloud before today."

It was a fittingly depressing way to end a frightfully depressing day.

Serafina swept quickly out the door, following in her brother's footsteps. Aidan was soon to follow, hoping to get some blood from the kitchens before they closed. Tanya stayed only long enough to comment on the pile of half-eaten figs before she, too, went off to sleep.

In the end it was only Katerina, Kailas, and Dylan who remained. An odd combination, but the day had been full of surprises.

"You want to know something strange?" Kailas pushed stiffly to his feet. "Two people died tonight on the castle grounds... and not one person thought to blame me."

Katerina glanced up in surprise, but could think of nothing to say. In terms of benchmarks, it was pretty sad. Then again, the prince had a lot of lost ground to cover.

That was *her* assessment. Others were not so generous.

"Congratulations, highness." Dylan's voice was flat. "What a milestone."

"Dylan," she chided quietly as Kailas blanched and looked at the floor.

"No, I'm serious." Dylan's eyes darkened, fixing on the door where Cassiel had disappeared just moments before. "Your father would be so proud. You know... if you hadn't..."

Katerina's mouth fell open in shock as her brother jerked back, looking as though he'd been burned. His chest rose with quick, shallow breaths, and before his sister could say a word to stop it he was on his feet, striding swiftly towards the door.

"You're right," he said softly, moving with a detached sort of grace. "If I hadn't slit his throat, I'm sure he would have been very proud. Goodnight, Katerina."

"Kailas—"

But he was already out the door.

Deprived of one target, she turned slowly to the other. Stunned almost to the point of speechlessness as her face whitened with rage.

"What the hell was that!"

Stunned *almost* to the point of speechlessness.

Dylan stared back impassively. Unmoved by the venom in her voice.

"I understand that you forgave him, but I can't." There was fire beneath the words that he was careful to control. "You'll find a lot of people around here can't. Take Kerien, for example."

The queen's eyes flashed at the injustice. "Oh, so that's how it's going to be? An endless ripple effect? Kailas killed Kerien—not some vengeful witch?"

"Yes, he might as well have."

"Dylan, that's ridiculously unfair—"

"We're all gathered here because of him. The five kingdoms are divided because of him. All this bloodshed, *everything* that..." He shook his head in frustration. "This is Damaris bloodshed."

The word hit her like a slap in the face. Just as powerful as Taviel, this one was taking on a whole different meaning. But it wasn't the death of the fae. It was the death of everyone.

Instead of arguing, she nodded and pushed gracefully to her feet. Instead of trying to change his mind, she deliberately straightened the crown on her head as she headed to the door.

"It seems these *peace* talks have come just in time."

He softened in spite of himself and pushed reluctantly to his feet, bowing his head with a quiet sigh. "Kat, I'm sorry. It's just—" A look of surprise flitted across his face when she cocked her head and pulled open the door. "Do you...do you want me to leave?"

She didn't say anything. She just stood there quietly until he decided she was serious, swiftly recovered himself, and gathered up his coat. Her head turned deliberately to the side as he walked past, and before he could say a word of goodnight she left him with some words of her own.

"When you're condemning my brother for his bloodline, just try to keep in mind that I'm a Damaris, too. And the dead king? Your punchline?"

Her eyes watered as she slammed the door.

"That was my father, too."

Chapter 9

By the time Katerina crawled into bed that night, it was only a few hours before dawn. The endless day had finally come to a close, but no matter how hard she tried the queen found herself unable to shut her eyes. Too many faces were parading past in the darkness. Too many unanswered questions were calling out her name.

How could everything have ended so badly? She stared unblinkingly at the ceiling. *With how much time we spent planning? With how long we had to prepare?*

Strangely enough, it wasn't the assassination attempt she was thinking about. It wasn't the missing vampire delegation, or even the fact that two of the diplomats had inexplicably died before properly digesting the cheese course. She was thinking about later. She was thinking about Dylan.

We've had so long to get used to the idea. He's had so long to get used to my name.

The first time the frightened queen had revealed she was actually the missing Damaris princess, she thought Dylan was going to walk away from her right then and there. Standing in the middle of the war-torn wilderness, ravaged by members of her own family, there seemed very little reason for him to stay. Even after he'd agreed. Even after he'd selflessly decided to dedicate himself to her cause, there had been a silent distance between them. An invisible wall keeping them apart. In the end, the only thing that had broken through was that they happened to fall madly in love.

But just being in love didn't erase decades of bloodshed and death. Loving her didn't mean he'd forgive the rest of her family. Forget the wretched curse of her name.

But Kailas was under a spell, she thought furiously. *What right does he have to hold that against him?*

A surge of anger bubbled up in her chest as she remembered the look on his face. As she replayed his exact words. *We're gathered here because of him. The five kingdoms are divided because of him. This is Damaris bloodshed.*

It was something about the way he said the word. The edge he gave to her name. It was as if he'd been able to compartmentalize it as long as it was just the two of them. As long as her twin stayed safely on his side of the castle; as long as the outside world kept its problems at bay.

But now all those problems were staring them right in the face. And with the discovery of two dead bodies in the course of one night, it was hard not to find a person toward whom to direct all that blame. Especially when the perfect person happened to be sitting just two seats down.

She didn't blame him. Even if she was angry. Even if he'd used the death of her father as a barb in Kailas' side. From the minute she'd found her brother chained up in that cell, she'd realized forgiveness would rest upon each person individually. They could not be swayed either way. Up until that evening, she had yet to fully embrace that forgiveness herself.

But still... Dylan heard what Kailas said. About wanting it to be over. About deserving to die. After hearing all that, after having felt that way himself, how could he possibly...

The covers went flying back as she pushed suddenly to her feet. Propelled with a fierce blaze of determination. Flickers of white hot rage dancing in her eyes.

No. HE doesn't get to be mad about this. HE has to be on my side. On my FAMILY'S side.

She tugged a silk robe out of her closet, stuffing her slender arms violently into the sleeves. It took a second of struggling to realize it was backwards before she yanked it the right way around.

The Damaris reign of terror is over. And Kailas and I were never even to blame! The perpetrators of all the bloodshed are dead and buried. The time for hating that name has come to an end.

The shoes were next. She found them only after a full minute of groping around in the dark.

And he's supposed to be my boyfriend! And a HALE—for bloody sake! If anyone should understand what it feels like to be blamed for the sins of one's family, it's HIM!

Long strands of fire-red hair trailed down her shoulders as she stomped to the door. Only partially aware of the fact that she was wearing two left shoes. The crown lay forgotten on her nightstand as she grabbed the handle and yanked it open with all her strength.

He'll just have to say he's sorry. He'll just have to apologize and find a way to make it—

"I'm sorry."

She froze in shock to see Dylan standing on the other side of the door. One hand still half-raised as he prepared to knock. He was in a similar state of undress, wearing only a loose white shirt and trousers, but was determined to get the words out before the door slammed in his face.

"Katerina, I apologize." His eyes shone with sincerity as they stared down into hers, silently asking for a second chance. "Please, let me find a way to make it right."

Suddenly, she was hyper-aware that she was wearing two ill-matching shoes. She was just as painfully aware that she'd forgotten to put a nightgown on beneath her robe. With as much dignity as she could possibly muster, she tossed back her hair and jutted up her chin. "Well... all right then."

He blinked, took a step forward, then froze. "All right?"

She shrugged. "What? You wanted a different answer?"

He stepped forward again, then caught himself staring with a hint of suspicion, like he was convinced it might be a trap. "You're just caving pretty fast, is all."

"I am not *caving*—"

"I was prepared to go fifty rounds, trying to win my way back into your good graces." He glanced at the floor next to him. "I brought water to rehydrate halfway through."

"You brought..." All that dignity disappeared with a cry of frustration. "Oh, that's it!" She grabbed him by the front of the shirt, tugging him through the door. "Get in here!"

"Well, should I bring the water, or—"

The door slammed shut behind him.

ONLY A FEW CANDLES were lit in the bedroom. Illuminating just their faces, while everything else was bathed in a silvery, moonlit glow.

"You are INFURIATING, do you know that?"

Katerina smacked Dylan as hard as she could in the chest, only to let out another frustrated cry as her robe slipped open, showing a flash of ivory skin just underneath. He opened his mouth for a staunch defense, but lost it immediately to a mischievous grin at the sight of her body.

"Katerina Damaris, I thought you were going to *scold* me."

The queen dropped her arms to her sides, staring at him in silence. He'd said her name right that time. Katerina Damaris. Not like an enemy—part of an ancient dynasty that could never be redeemed. But as a fire-breathing teenage dragon. The girl he'd fallen in love with in the woods.

"I can scold you," she answered quietly.

She was still angry. Sheesh, she still was *furious*. But she didn't need a showdown between the queen of the High Kingdom and the king of Belaria. She needed the ranger. She needed her friend.

He instantly registered her change of tone and the mischief faded away. It was replaced with a tired sort of remorse. One that had taken little bits of him every hour he'd been away.

"There's no need." His bowed head with a sigh. "I've done well enough all by myself."

With a forced maturity beyond their years, the weary couple sank onto the edge of the mattress. Cautious, at first. Inching closer and closer, until at last they were in each other's arms.

"I couldn't sleep," Dylan confessed. "I kept replaying every word. Remembering the look on your face when you told me to leave." His chest tightened and he shot her a sideways look. "You've never done that before. Wanted me to go."

Katerina glared up at him defiantly, pulling out of his arms. "Well, you've never made a joke about the death of my father. You've never accused my brother of killing someone he's never even met—"

"You're right," Dylan said quickly, holding up his hands. "I absolutely deserved it."

They gave each other a measured stare before slowly coming together once more.

"I just... hated it," he continued softly. "I hated myself. Knowing that you were in here by yourself—hurting. That I'd done that to you."

Katerina bit her lip, staring fixedly at the floor. *He said he was sorry. He said he wanted to make it right. He said that he deserved to go.*

...but he never said he was wrong.

She glanced up at his face, staring a moment at those beautiful starlit eyes, before venturing a tentative question. A question she wasn't sure she even wanted to ask.

"You really hate him, don't you? You really can't forgive him?"

Every muscle in his body stiffened as Dylan pulled in a silent breath.

He would do anything in the world for the girl sitting next to him. He would give his own life if the fates demanded it. But forgiving the man who'd hurt her so deeply? Who'd hurt the world?

He didn't want to lie to her. In the end, he answered as honestly as he could.

"I can try."

Her eyes shot up in surprise, and before he could pull in a breath she'd circled his neck with her tiny arms. "Really?" she whispered. "You would actually try? For me?"

A knot hardened in his chest, but he breathed through it. Forcing a smile. "For you."

Anything. For you.

Just like that, the argument was over.

They'd never been good at fighting with one another. It didn't help that one had the tendency to breathe fire, while the other spontaneously shifted into a wolf. They were doing the best they could.

Two teenagers with the weight of five kingdoms on their heads.

After a few minutes of silence, a little grin pulled up at the corners of Katerina's mouth as she fiddled with the front of her robe. "You know, I'm not exactly wearing anything under this..."

Dylan forgot about one twin completely, pulling the other into his arms. "Is that right?"

The two came together for a gentle kiss. Fingers lacing through fingers. Messy hair stained silver in the light of the moon. Just one kiss, then they curled together in the center of the bed. Her head resting on his shoulder. His arm circled around her waist. It was the way they'd fallen asleep every night since returning to the castle. The only brightness in an otherwise cloudy day.

"Dylan," she whispered a few minutes later, wondering if he'd fallen asleep, "you awake?"

His arms tightened and he pressed a gentle kiss to her forehead.

"What do you think we're going to be talking about tomorrow?" she asked. "Do you think it's all going to focus on the investigation? Or will they wait on Petra for that?"

Dylan sighed quietly, curling his fingers into her fiery hair. "If I know anything about royal politics, I imagine we're going to forget the body count all together and pick up right where we left off—fighting for peace."

KATERINA HAD ONLY BEEN awake a few seconds before she realized something was wrong. Just a few seconds, but she had already gone and done the one thing she always swore she wouldn't.

She'd woken up in Dylan's arms.

...Crap!

It was one thing to fall asleep with him. The entire realm already knew the two were secretly dating. But as beloved as both young monarchs were, this was never meant to be an adolescent romance. Such a thing was not allowed. There were kingdoms at stake. And for the sake of those kingdoms, certain appearances had to be upheld.

A late night could be explained away. But an early morning?

That implied something else entirely...

"Dylan," she whispered frantically, trying to squirm her way free. *"Dylan, wake up!"*

Her back was fitted snugly against his bare chest, and a tan, muscular arm was draped lightly across her waist. It tightened when she said his name. Pulling her closer, the way a child would hug a stuffed bear. But he didn't open his eyes.

"Honey, wake up! It's morning!"

They had been careful, thus far. So very careful. Dylan might have laid down with her every night since the battle, but he was never there when she awoke the next morning. There was an imprint in the sheets.

Maybe a flower on the pillow if he was feeling especially sweet. But most of the time, he was simply gone.

She would get dressed, untangle the incriminating knots in her hair, and head downstairs to the dining room for breakfast. At that point, she would greet him for the 'first time.' At *that* point, the servants would giggle and roll their eyes.

They'd been impeccable about keeping up the charade, but yesterday's activities proved too much for the young king. Between the banquet, the deaths, the assassination attempt, and the fact that he'd only climbed into bed an hour or so earlier, he was still fast asleep.

"Dylan—"

"Quiet," he murmured, blindly cupping his hand over her lips. "Sleep time."

She wrenched his hand away, stifling a giggle whilst casting nervous glances to the door at the same time. "Sleep time's done, babe. It's morning. Time to get up."

He rolled onto his stomach, pressing his face into the pillow. "You talk too much. We're breaking up until you learn not to talk so much."

The pillow was yanked away. His head fell unceremoniously onto the mattress.

"What was that?"

He pried open first one eye, then another—squinting into the bright sunlight as his girlfriend towered over him, arms folded over her chest. He considered carefully, then revised. "I said... good morning?"

Damn right.

"*It is morning*," she said for the third time, directing his gaze towards the window. "They'll be serving breakfast soon; I'm sure the hallways are already flooded with dignitaries. You've got to get out of here before—"

There was a sharp knock on the door.

—before that.

The couple froze in perfect unison, then stared anxiously at the door. Nothing happened for a moment, then it seemed to rattle on its hinges as someone knocked again.

"You Majesty, might I have a word?"

Dylan's eyes snapped shut as his head dropped back upon the pillow. "Crap," he breathed. "It's Atticus."

The head of the Belarian Council had come to make sure that his king was awake and ready for the start of the summit. And he'd come to *Katerina's* room to find him.

"What should we do?" Katerina whispered.

Dylan pressed a quick finger to his lips, then tapped twice on his ear. The silent message was received and understood. Shifters could hear everything. And Atticus was more talented than most.

So where does that leave us?

The young king considered for a moment, glancing down at his naked chest, before his eyes drifted towards the long curtains on the far wall. "I could go out the window..."

Katerina could have sworn he only mouthed the words, but no sooner had he done so than an amused (if somewhat exasperated) voice drifted through the door.

"Very resourceful, my lord, but I'm afraid you'll find the kitchen staff is already setting up for an afternoon picnic on the lawn. And as much as I'm sure they'd appreciate the show, perhaps you could simply put on some clothes and speak with me for a moment."

Katerina blushed a million shades of scarlet, while Dylan went perfectly still.

It was a bold move—for a councilman to address his monarch in such a way. Especially when said monarch had yet to find his pants. But Atticus and Dylan didn't exactly have a typical relationship when it came to such things. They never had.

Atticus was the man who'd warned the Hale family to run for their lives. The same man who'd launched a two-year search for the missing prince. He'd watched over Dylan since the day he was born. Seen him take his first steps. Looked down from a palace window as he mounted his first horse. Taught him how to properly nock an arrow and aim high to hit the target. Had Dylan been living in Belaria during his first transformation, Atticus would have guided him through that as well.

No, they didn't have the typical monarch-subject relationship. While Katerina knew he'd never admit such a thing, she was sure the councilman thought of Dylan as a surrogate son. And fathers could speak in such a bold manner to their sons.

...especially when their son woke up in the wrong maiden's bed.

The game was up, and this time Dylan didn't bother to lower his voice. He simply gritted his teeth and banged his head lightly against the wall. "Why did I ever come back..."

"Take your time, sire," Atticus replied cheerfully. "I'm happy to wait."

Even through a cloud of mortification, Katerina was able to see the humor. She watched with a secret grin as Dylan pushed himself out of bed and rummaged around on the floor for his clothes. Shook with silent laughter as he struggled to find his shoes, then gave up on the notion entirely. Hid behind the door as he cracked it open with a bloodshot glare.

"Good morning, Atticus. Fancy meeting you here."

The two shared a long look, one that dropped incriminatingly to His Majesty's bare feet, before the councilman stepped forward with a tight smile.

"May I come in, sire?" He cocked his head ever-so-slightly towards the bustling hallway behind him. "Unless you'd prefer to speak in public?"

For a split second, it looked like Dylan would rise to the challenge. Then his eyes flickered to a cluster of giggling maids and he pulled open the door further, allowing the councilman inside.

It was a good thing that Katerina had anticipated such a maneuver. She was already dressed and sitting behind her desk, surely going over state documents and such.

"Good morning, Atticus," she said brightly. "We were just headed down for breakfast."

The man offered her a polite, if somewhat strained, smile. "Were you now," he replied cordially before turning to Dylan. "And what were you doing before that, pray tell?"

Dylan never blinked, matching him stare for stare. "Working."

Atticus' eyes drifted to the desk. Katerina shuffled some papers around for good measure.

"Your Majesties," he began with a quiet sigh, "may I have permission to speak freely?"

"Of course," Katerina replied instantly.

"No," Dylan countered at the same time.

The king received two chiding looks before Atticus softly cleared his throat.

"There isn't a person in the five kingdoms who doesn't know how the two of you feel about each other. I was able to sense it from the minute you stepped inside the castle doors. Even worn from your travels, even bound in chains, I could see you loved each other."

Katerina's heart quickened as Dylan went very pale. They had danced around the issue since their grand return, but no one had mentioned it directly. Not until now.

"Please just—" Dylan cut himself off quickly, eyes flashing ever so briefly to his girlfriend before returning to Atticus with a silent plea. "Can we not do this now?"

The councilman's eyes softened sympathetically, but he shook his head. "I'm afraid there's no putting it off any longer. Your presence in Belaria has been deeply missed, sire, and now that representatives from all five kingdoms have come for the summit, it's time to call this what it is."

And what is that? Katerina thought fearfully. *What exactly is he calling this?*

"A personal matter that's none of your concern?" Dylan offered angrily.

"It's *out* of your control," the councilman replied softly.

For some reason, despite the numerous things he could have said, this simple statement was somehow more powerful than all the rest. Not that they shouldn't do it. Not that it wasn't wise. But that it wasn't in their hands in the first place. They had been fooling themselves all along.

But that didn't mean they weren't going to try...

"And what would be wrong with it?" Dylan growled. It had taken all his patience and strength just to get used to the castle carpet. Katerina couldn't imagine what it was taking for him to frame his love life in political terms now. "She is a queen, I am a king. The five kingdoms have gathered to make alliances and secure the peace. They should be thrilled that we—"

"Yes, there are *five* kingdoms that have gathered together, my lord," Atticus interrupted with a touch of impatience. "And under no circumstances would they be thrilled by such a match."

The room fell suddenly quiet as the teenagers stared back at him in shock. Neither one understanding. Neither one remotely prepared for such a turn of events.

But while Dylan was merely angry, Katerina saw something else in the councilman's eyes.

"You've already discussed this, haven't you?" she asked with sudden certainty. "You and your people. The Kreo, the Fae. My own council." Her hands clenched with a thrill of dread. "This has already been discussed."

Atticus bowed his head with a sigh, suddenly looking much older than his forty years.

"Of course it's been discussed," he said quietly. "It's been discussed since the moment Dylan set foot back on royal soil. Since the moment Kailas stepped down and you ascended the throne."

This statement was met with even more shock.

"But... when?" Dylan asked in a daze. "And why didn't you tell me? I've been—"

"I've been doing nothing *but* telling you," Atticus replied. "Warning you from the moment you decided to stay in the High Kingdom. Cautioning you to keep your distance from that girl."

That girl didn't take kindly to the moniker, but at the moment both she and Dylan were too distracted to care. Truth be told, they hadn't expected anyone to actually take issue with their secret romance. They'd been discreet out of political courtesy. But to hear Atticus frame it in such terms?

"Why would anyone have a problem with it?" Katerina asked quietly. "If Dylan and I were to..." She blushed and lowered her eyes. "Why would it be a problem?"

Atticus looked on them both with great pity. "Because it's been done before."

They froze a moment in confusion, but he carried on before either could speak.

"Which realms allied themselves in the Great War? Which peoples have spent decades fighting together for the same cause? Belaria and the High Kingdom."

An icy shiver swept down Katerina's spine as he answered his own question.

"The Damaris and Hale dynasties wreaked destruction on the rest of the world standing side by side. Is it any small wonder the five kingdoms wouldn't want to make a similar alliance now?"

The whole speech came off much sharper than was intended, and Atticus took a deliberate step back, leaving the two shell-shocked teenagers standing in his wake. A full minute passed, but neither could think of anything to say. In the end, Katerina simply bowed her head with a quiet,

"Oh."

So that's the reason. The dark truth none of our council has been willing to say.

"I didn't think..." Dylan trailed off, looking as lost as she'd ever seen him. "I didn't think something like that would apply to us. Not after what we..." He trailed off again, looking both outmaneuvered and unexpectedly sad. "But I understand why they'd feel that way."

Katerina's eyes flashed up, but she held her tongue. In a way, she was happy he'd been the one to say it first. Yes, on paper, a Damaris-Hale alliance was an ominous echo of the atrocities both families had committed in the past. She could understand an initial reluctance to commit.

But she and Dylan had spent their lives *fighting* that legacy. Didn't that count for anything?

"I just assumed..." Dylan's eyes flickered up to Atticus before he dropped them again with a sigh. "I mean, we're here for royal peace negotiations. I just assumed marriage proposals would automatically be on the table."

"You did?" Katerina asked sharply.

She had as well, but they'd made very sure not to talk about it. There were only so many things that this forced maturity of theirs could cover. Sure enough, he met her gaze only for one terrified moment before looking quickly at the floor.

"No," he denied automatically. "I mean... yes. Didn't you?"

"No," she scoffed dismissively. Then a far milder, "...but it would make sense."

"Oh, children."

Both their heads snapped up at once to see Atticus staring at them, one hand covering his mouth. If Katerina thought he'd looked sympathetic before, it was nothing compared to the gut-wrenching pity on his face now. It passed from one to the other, shining in his eyes.

"You misunderstand me," he said quietly, looking too mortified for words. There was a heavy pause before he forced himself to continue. "Marriage proposals are *very much* on the table."

Chapter 10

There was no time to tell anyone. Things were moving too fast. No sooner had Dylan and Katerina wrapped their heads around what Atticus was trying to tell them, than they were whisked out the door by an array of servants. It didn't matter that the two teenagers were stunned past the point of speech. No one seemed to notice the way they were staring unblinkingly at the floor, looking like they'd been trapped in a bad dream.

They were dressed and pressed and escorted down the stairs to the council hall. Since they'd missed the royal breakfast, tiny pastries and cups of cider were pressed into their hands. When it became clear they had no intention of eating, they were quickly removed and tossed along the way.

The last thing Katerina remembered was a pair of unseen hands pressing the crown atop her head as she was shoved through the double doors and into the main chamber.

The room went quiet. A hundred pairs of eyes turned to stare. She and Dylan froze in the entryway as she began to silently recite the same three words.

Do. Not. Cry.

With an ingrained nobility that ran in their very blood, they lifted their chins and walked to the raised dais at the end of the room. Moving with muscle memory. Hardly feeling their feet.

The rest of their friends were already seated. Looking calm but predictably uncomfortable under the enormous spotlight. The rest of the tables were angled in a strange circle—doming outward, so everyone could see each other but stay facing the monarchs at the same time. One delegation was at each table. One kingdom represented by the highest legates in the land. The table of vampires remained empty, but at the moment it was the lowest concern.

Things were about to get terrible. Their every nightmare was about to come to life.

As Katerina took a seat beside Tanya, the shape-shifter leaned over with a chiding grin. "So you may have been royalty a lot longer than me, but missing a royal breakfast? Rookie move."

The queen couldn't respond. Couldn't even look at her. Couldn't unglue her tongue from the top of her mouth. She simply sat there, counting down the seconds until her beloved Tanya's smile would melt away. Until she would be feeling the same way, too.

"Ladies and gentlemen, thank you all for coming." The head of her own council, Abel Bishop, pushed back his chair to take them through the basic preliminaries. "Before we begin, I'd like to offer my sincere condolences for the events of last night. The prayers of the five kingdoms are with the families. Rest assured, the perpetrators will be found and brought to justice."

His words were met with resounding silence.

The delegation of Fae had discarded their usual creams and silvers for matching cloaks of black. A color of mourning that Cassiel was wearing as well.

Katerina stared at them silently, wondering why they'd thought to bring funeral clothes at all.

"In the meantime, we must honor their sacrifice and remember the reason we are here." His eyes scanned over the room, looking at each table in turn. "To forge a strong and lasting peace."

This, at least, produced a reaction. Quite murmurs of assent echoed from every corner of the great hall. Even the witches, who were looking decidedly worse for wear, couldn't help but agree.

"Which brings us to the first item on the agenda. Although a bit strange to discuss in such a wide forum, the oldest method of allying neighboring kingdoms has always proven the best."

There was a slight pause.

"That is, marriage."

This time, the reaction was much louder. It seemed the one thing the quarrelling people of the five kingdoms could agree on was that their young monarchs should take each other's hand in marriage. People of every culture and kingdom were nodding their heads, adding their own voice of consent as the idea travelled quickly around the room.

But for the first time, they weren't the only ones with an opinion.

Katerina glanced from side to side, only to see that her friends had clearly been expecting this kind of news themselves. And although it broke her heart, it wasn't entirely unwelcome.

Tanya was looking confident. Aidan was looking thoughtful. Cassiel was staring at the empty chair where his friend would have sat.

Only Dylan was looking decidedly shaken. Staring unblinkingly at the floor. As if he alone already knew that the battle had been fought and lost.

"At this time," Bishop continued, "I would like to open the floor. If any of the parties gathered would care to speak, they are free to do so now."

There was a quiet commotion amongst the tables. An electric buzz of conversation as a dozen hushed voices started speaking all at once. Katerina braced in her chair, wondering who was going to speak first. Where it was going to come from. Then, before Bishop had even sat down, another chair pulled back as Leonor, head council of the Fae, pushed gracefully to his feet.

The Fae may have lost a cherished representative to a freak homicide, but they were in no way diminished. Leonor stood tall and serene, his voice ringing authoritatively across the room.

"On behalf of Cassiel Elénarin, last of the High Born and prince of the Fae, we would like to extend an offer of marriage... to Katerina Damaris."

You could have heard a pin drop.

Nobody moved. Not a single person. A cold sheen of sweat broke out over Katerina's forehead and, seated on either side, both Dylan and Tanya had gone very still.

Only Cassiel lifted his head, looking like he was coming out of a daze.

"...wh-what?"

There was movement in the room. Leonor's calm façade faltered. He shot a quick backwards glance at the rest of his party before clearing his throat. "My lord, it was discussed and—"

"Not by me," Cassiel interrupted, pushing abruptly to his feet. "It was not discussed by me."

Dylan had eyes only for his girlfriend and Katerina was sinking slowly in her chair. Watching her world get smaller and smaller as the walls started closing in.

The fae were stirring restlessly. The other delegations looked on with wary eyes. But Cassiel was having none of it. Perhaps it was because he'd lost a friend. Perhaps it was because he'd been kept up all night by his bird. But the dignified woodland prince vanished before Katerina's very eyes.

"My apologies," he nodded curtly to the rest of the room, "but my councilman is mistaken. There is no offer of marriage between Katerina and myself."

If only it was that simple. But he hadn't been there for Atticus' speech.

"My *lord*." There was a dangerous edge to Leonor's voice, one that made the hairs on the back of Katerina's neck stand on end. "There will be time enough to discuss this later—"

"I will not marry her," Cassiel repeated in a clear voice. "A mortal child? Who will make me a widower in sixty years' time? I think not."

Tanya flinched at the word *widower* as Dylan leaned back in his chair. As for Katerina? She was lost in a distant memory. One that was more and more painfully ironic by the minute.

Back at the Talsing monastery, she and Cassiel had joked about how it might have been if life had been different and the two of them had been betrothed. He'd graciously promised to be a wonderful husband, as long as she gave him permission to cheat. They'd laughed about it then.

But things were different now...

"If there are to be proposals of marriage, perhaps it would be best for the delegations to first speak with the persons themselves." Atticus pushed tentatively to his feet. Possibly because he'd witnessed a similar reaction just ten minutes earlier in Katerina's room; possibly because he was physically afraid of the look on Dylan's face. "We could adjourn for a short recess—"

"Why?" asked a particularly heartless shifter. "The pairs have already been decided. The queen will marry the fae. Our king will marry his sister. And the crown prince and the queen of the Kreo will be married as well. Five kingdoms united. That is... unless the vampires offer a candidate."

It took a second for the words to register. Then the entire head table pushed to its feet.

"Me?" Kailas asked in surprise. "You say I'm to marry Tanya?"

He had obviously thought he fell firmly into the category of 'damaged goods.' The same way that Serafina had assumed the second in line to the throne would be exempt from such discussion.

But royalty was in short supply. Concessions would have to be made.

"Not in a million years," Tanya hissed under her breath. "A million freakin' years."

Dissention was like a plague, and it didn't take long for the rest of the room to start yelling. A select few people had known about this game of marital chairs, and everyone who was hearing about it for the first time seemed to have their own opinion. But none more so than the people in question.

Tempers flared as the volume swelled to a deafening roar. Dwarves were standing on tables just to be better heard. Nymphs and witches were demanding they get a marriage contract of their own. A lone voice from the back of the room cautioned that the vampires would want to have their say, and by the time *that* idea circled around the place was in a complete uproar.

Only Katerina was still sitting at the table. Pale as a sheet and frozen unnaturally still.

Me and Cassiel? Kailas and Tanya?

...Dylan and Serafina?

Her eyes flashed with a quiet sort of panic as that telltale fire started burning in her chest. The cold sweat was replaced with a hot flush as her hands clenched sporadically by her sides.

"Kat?"

Only Aidan noticed her distress, everyone else caught up in the madness sweeping over the council hall. He slipped quietly from his chair and knelt by her side, taking her hand in his.

"Sweetheart, control it." He spoke quietly, giving her a gentle squeeze. "You *must* control it."

Never did he use such terms of endearment. Just a single time when she was bleeding to death in a swamp. Vampires tended to shy away from such emotional attachments, and it took a lot for him to slip into one now.

"Katerina," he cautioned again. "Take a breath."

His cool hand flinched when it came in contact with her burning skin. The tips of her fingers were beginning to smoke. But as much as she wanted to listen to him, as much as she wanted to honor his request, things had spiraled out of her control.

"I can't..." she whispered, pushing her chair away from the table, "I can't do this."

He stood up with her, casting an anxious look around the hall. To shift in a closed space, so densely populated, would be catastrophic. Not to the queen, but to everyone else unfortunate enough to be in the room. He had seen the dragon firsthand. It did not play well with others.

"Two seconds," he murmured, sweeping her legs out from under her and lifting her into his arms. "Just two seconds—do you trust me?"

She closed her eyes and nodded. Trying hard to breathe. Trying hard to control the unquenchable fire raging in her chest. Yes, she could give him two seconds. She trusted him.

A rush of wind blew back her hair, hitting her face with enough force to make it sting. Her eyes watered as she opened them, only to find that the room had disappeared. They were both outside now. Standing in an open field of grass.

"There..." Aidan backed slowly away, watching her all the while. "It's safe now."

She didn't have time to thank him. She didn't even have time to smile. It was exactly two seconds later, and that was all the time she had to spare.

There was a high-pitched shriek as her body ripped apart in a whirlwind of flames. A second later, a crimson dragon rose up in her place. Dripping with fire. Spreading its enormous wings.

The crown fell with a thud onto the grass.

Thank you.

The two locked eyes, and although she was beyond the point of words there wasn't a doubt in her mind that Aidan could understand. He always did. Somehow.

He nodded once and picked up her fallen crown.

What others bowed to with such reverence he tossed carelessly from hand to hand, the corner of his mouth twitching up with a little smile.

"I'll just hold on to this, shall I?"

The queen flashed a grin, then launched herself into the air. Spiraling up through the clouds in a writhing ball of fire. Leaving the mess at the castle far behind. Closing her eyes, her wings caught the wind like the sail of a ship, carrying her off into the horizon.

IT WAS NIGHTFALL BY the time Katerina returned. She hadn't meant to stay away so long, but it was hard to keep track of such things as a dragon. At any rate, she probably wouldn't have come back. The freedom of flight was addictive, and she'd been denied it for much too long.

Her powerful wings beat in a steady, tireless rhythm as she circled the kingdom, moving in a slow orbit with the sun. Those latent muscles ached from lack of use, and stretched out with the greatest delight as she skimmed the surface of the clouds. Wondering why she hadn't done it long ago. Wondering why she spent all her time locked in a castle instead.

Dylan had tried to explain once how it felt when he forced himself to remain in human form for too long. The claustrophobic restlessness when he caged the wolf inside. She hadn't understood. She'd been just a girl then, roaming about with him in the wild without the faintest idea as to the raw power secretly coursing through her own veins.

She'd always wondered what it would be like to shift. To feel her body tear apart and transform itself into something new. She'd always wondered if it hurt.

He'd promised that it didn't. He'd told her it was one of the most amazing sensations in the world—second only to sex. Dylan always added things like that. And always with a wink.

Her lips curled up in a smile as she remembered. Yes, it wouldn't be a 'Dylan' explanation if it didn't end by making her blush. But that was the man she'd fallen in love with. The man she'd recently abandoned in a screaming council hall...

The picnic tents had been put away. The guards had switched to the night shift, and for the most part things were quiet as she dove silently through the clouds and alighted on the roof. In the beginning, it had been hard for her to put away the dragon and shift back into the queen. That first transformation back in the woods had been terrifying. Now, it was as easy as taking a breath.

The shimmering scales fell away as a lovely fire-haired girl appeared in their midst. She stood there for a second, getting her bearings, before moving quickly to a chest of clothes she'd snuck onto the parapet for just such an occasion. Inside was a pile of dresses and cloaks. She took the simplest one, slipped it over her head, and climbed down quickly to her bedroom window.

She had an idea someone might be waiting...

"Kat."

Dylan called out the second her body swung in through the window, landing lightly on the floor. Sure enough—he'd been perched upon one of her bookshelves, immersed in medieval history anthology that weighed as much as her. He slipped a knife between the pages to mark his place, dropping to the floor with the grace of a cat. A second later, she was standing in his arms.

"Aidan told me what happened," he murmured, running his fingers through her hair. "I'm sorry I didn't take you myself. I was... diplomatting."

Katerina smiled as he used Tanya's favorite new word. Yes, he'd been in the middle of 'diplomatting' when she'd left. She was surprised the castle was still standing.

"I'm sorry to just take off—"

"Don't be," he interrupted gently, shaking it off as if people escaped into the sky as dragons all the time. "I'm glad you did. I would have done it myself if I didn't think I'd be married-by-proxy to some goblin duchess by the time I got back."

Katerina flinched at the words, then couldn't help but grin. "...do goblins have duchesses?"

He pulled back with a grave expression, tucking a lock of hair behind her ear. "In some of my darker dreams."

She laughed aloud, gazing up at him. For a girl who'd never placed much stock in the idea of true love, she'd fallen hard. Losing herself completely. Finding herself as well. Devoting every waking breath to the beautiful man in her bedroom. Surrendering herself, body and soul.

Then her mind flashed to that terrible morning and her smile faded.

"What happened after I left?" she asked quietly.

His whole body flinched. This from a man who didn't flinch easily. "It wasn't good—" he began, then shook his head. "Nothing. Let's not...let's not even talk about it." She looked up at him fearfully, but he stroked her cheek with a warm smile. "I can think of quite a few better things we could do with our time."

Before she knew what was happening, she was lying on the bed. Hair splayed out over the pillows. His body pressed lightly atop hers.

Dylan did things suddenly. It was one of the things she liked about him best.

"*Now*?" she gasped as he pressed his lips to her neck. "Honey, don't you think we should maybe talk about what happened?"

The first time she'd called him honey, he hadn't known what to make of it. Now, it never failed to produce a smile.

"What's there to talk about?" he asked between kisses, already compartmentalizing and blocking the rest of it out. "As far as I'm concerned there's only you and me, and—"

"—and the fact that I'm betrothed to your best friend?"

There was a rush of cold air as he swiftly pulled away.

For just a fleeting moment, she was able to see a crack in the armor. For just a fleeting moment, she witnessed the war of emotions dancing behind those blue eyes. Then he flashed her a quick smile and shook his head. Proceeding as if nothing had happened.

"You're not betrothed. You never agreed." He kissed her deliberately. Forcefully. As if he could make their problems go away simply by willing it so. "I would never let that happen."

She wanted to believe him. She wanted it *so badly*. But there was a reason Dylan had forsaken royal life in the first place. Because it put you in situations where things were beyond your control.

"We might not have a choice—"

"You are *mine*," he interrupted fiercely.

She startled at the sudden ferocity in his voice, and he took her face gently between his hands. Their eyes locked and the rest of the world seemed to fall away.

"I am yours, and you are mine," he repeated, softer this time. Those blue eyes softened with a look of tender adoration. "And nothing...*nothing* is ever going to change that. You have my word."

They stared for one suspended moment. Then she nodded with a smile.

He had never failed her. Not once. Not matter how bleak their chances. No matter how impossible the task. He had never once failed her when he'd given his word.

Her smile coaxed one of his own, and a second later she was pulling him back down for another kiss. Their bodies came together quickly, easily. Like they'd been designed specifically to do so.

His fingers untangled the ribbons lacing up her back as she slid his shirt over his head. Her hands traced the muscles in his chest as he eased the sleeves of her dress off her shoulders. Just a few seconds later, they were both lying naked in the bed. Tangled together. Locked in a passionate embrace, a delicate balance of frantic breathing and careful restraint.

...or not so much restraint?

Katerina froze as his hand disappeared beneath the covers, gently parting her knees. Her eyes flashed up to his, but he was in a whole other world. Eyes closed, kissing her between shallow breaths, dark hair brushing across her forehead as he hitched her legs around his waist.

"Dylan," she gasped, leaning back into the pillow, gazing up at him in surprise, "what are you doing?"

"What does it look like?" He bit playfully at her ear, eyes dancing with a wicked grin. "I'm trying to seduce my girlfriend."

Her body froze, but her mind was racing a thousand miles a minute. Despite having spent every night together, despite having enjoyed each other very much, there were certain lines they were careful never to cross. It hadn't been her choice, but his. He'd wanted to 'do it right.' At the proper time, in the proper place. So that her first time was everything it deserved to be.

She'd hated him for it. And loved him all the more.

But he picks tonight?

Unable to think of another option, she decided to stall.

"It's just," she twisted her head away, squeezing in words between his kisses, "the last queen you tried to sleep with... well, you ended up setting her castle on fire."

He pulled back in surprise, then let out a bark of laughter.

"Please," he scoffed, "that was just foreplay. Besides, I happen to like your castle." He pulled her closer with a grin. "I like it here very much..."

Then he kissed her again and she forgot all her reservations.

This was finally going to happen? Perfect—she'd been waiting for a *very* long time. She wrapped her hand around the back of his neck and pulled herself up higher on the pillows. There was a hitch in his breathing, and for just a moment she looked up into those beautiful sky-blue eyes.

...and froze.

Because, as much as it killed her, she saw another face. Wet hair, trembling hands and wide, nervous eyes. Staring down at her in a Kreo bath house, all those months ago.

I want to do this right with you. Would something like that be possible?

He'd wanted to wait then and he wanted to wait now, even if he didn't realize it himself.

This was not that perfect moment he'd described—after the leaders of the land had declared she should marry someone else. This was a panicked reaction. This was not 'doing it right.'

"I thought we were going to wait," she whispered, pulling back once more.

"I don't want to wait," he breathed, tangling his fingers in her hair. "I want to do this. *Now.*"

No, you don't, my love.

She placed a hand on the side of his face, forcing him to look her in the eyes. "Dylan."

He stared at her for a moment, then bowed his head with a quiet sigh. "Kiss me, then."

That she was more than willing to do.

Her eyes filled with tears as she pulled them together. Crying, when he could not. Feeling the panic, when he wouldn't allow himself. Taking silent solace in the strong embrace of his arms.

They kissed for a long time. Holding on to each other in the dark.

But even his kisses scared her. They were different than before. Urgent. Like every kiss was numbered. Like he was worried they might not get another chance...

Chapter 11

The summit was suspended, further negotiations put on hold. It was 'out of respect for the dead.' That was the reason Abel Bishop gave at breakfast the next morning. The actual reason was rather transparent. The summit was suspended until six reluctant teenagers could be coerced into marrying each other. Only the vampire was exempt. He was cheerfully neutral either way.

"Why doesn't Aidan have to deal with any of this?" Katerina complained as she and Dylan crept down the hallway the next morning. They'd set out well before dawn so as not to be seen. "It's ridiculously unfair. He's just free to do whatever he wants."

"That's because no one wants to marry a vampire." Dylan grabbed the back of her dress and pulled her quickly behind a suit of armor, just as a trio of shifters came back from a morning jog. As soon as they were past, the couple crept forward once more. "Even our own councils would never stoop so low as to suggest it. They'd just demand we ruin our lives some other way."

Unable to process his fatalism until she was caffeinated, Katerina ignored this and moved on. "That's absolutely ridiculous! I can understand some trepidation about vampires in general, but this is Aidan we're talking about. You've seen how the women in the castle look at him. Plus he's kind, and insightful, and who the heck *wouldn't* want to marry him."

"You know I hate it when you talk like that."

Dylan was only half-joking, but the two of them shared a grin.

Since the queen and the vampire had forged a special blood connection deep in the Kreo jungle, her boyfriend had been trying to keep his jealousy at bay. Aidan had only done it to save her life, and he himself had offered his blood as tribute later that same night.

But the young king didn't exactly like to share his toys, and the fact that the two had gotten abnormally close grated occasionally on his nerves. Even more so because he was never able to get properly angry, as he'd grown impossibly fond of the vampire himself.

"Deplorable little leech," he muttered, pushing open the door to the council hall. "I should have done away with him when I had the—"

The couple froze in the doorway.

"—chance."

They had come to the grand council hall, because it was the last place any of the councilmen would think to look for them. The place they *should* be avoiding like the plague.

Ironically enough, it seemed the others had the same idea...

"What are you guys doing here?" Tanya demanded through a mouthful of biscuit.

She was reclining lazily in Katerina's throne, leaning against an armrest with her legs thrown over the other side. For good measure, she'd also stolen the crown from Aidan. It was tilted precariously on her head, held up by the jagged spikes of her mohawk.

Katerina moved forward with a grin, stealing a cup of cider from Kailas on the way. "What have I told you about eating in my chair?"

The shape-shifter smiled, sucking honey off the tips of her fingers, one by one. "You said that you'd strongly consider it."

There was a chorus of laughter and Katerina was about to reply, when she found herself lifted into the air by a pair of strong arms. Fully expecting Dylan, she was absolutely stunned when it was Cassiel who spun her around, holding her tenderly against his chest.

"Good morning." He kissed her softly on the cheek, lingering a second too long, before kissing the other as well. "I have to admit... I couldn't stop thinking about you last night."

Katerina's body froze as she stared up at him in shock. "You... what?"

"I was surprised myself." His eyes twinkled as he stroked a finger along her lower lip, trying very hard not to smile. "You know, I might have been too hasty yesterday before the council. There might be an actual chance that you and I could make this work—"

There was a snort of laughter, then the gang erupted once more.

"Oh, come on!" Cassiel glanced over his shoulder with a scowl. "I had at least three more things I was planning to say."

"Okay. Very funny." Dylan pulled her away with a rueful grin, wrapping his own arms tightly around her waist. "I'm glad to see you've kept a sense of humor, what with Kailas Damaris screwing your little sister every night."

Cassiel's smile faded as Serafina piped up from atop the podium.

"Leave me out of this."

"Me, too," Kailas added under his breath.

"I think Dylan's just jealous of your moves," Tanya inserted helpfully. "That was some quality work, babe. You've really got that whole smoldering thing down."

"I wasn't nearly finished," Cassiel replied crossly. "Katerina—come here."

Dylan swatted his outstretched hand out of the air. "New plan. How about I turn into a wolf and rip you to pieces?"

The fae smiled sweetly. "Aw, your little dog trick? You'd do that for me?"

"How the heck did I end up with you people?" Aidan muttered with a grin.

"The question is, how did you people all end up *here*?" Katerina intervened, steering them back on point. "The main council hall? Really?"

"It's the last place anyone would think to look," Tanya answered practically before throwing the remains of the biscuit at her with a grin. "*You* came here, didn't you?"

"Yeah, but Dylan and I are a lot smarter than the rest of you." Katerina settled cross-legged at her feet. "What were you guys talking about anyway? Everyone was so weird when we came in."

Tanya lit up with a smile, casting her boyfriend a mischievous grin. "I was just asking Sera how it was that two people locked away in a dungeon happened to fall madly in love."

Cassiel closed his eyes with a pained grimace. "Which is a story we absolutely do *not* need to hear. Can't we just chalk it up to psychological trauma and be done?"

"Absolutely," Dylan agreed swiftly.

But the girls weren't so quick to let it go. In fact, Katerina found herself highly interested in the answer. She had only recently discovered that her brother was capable of human emotion, and his newfound romance happened under stranger circumstances than most. She remembered the way Alwyn had taunted them both in the dungeon. How they were so close, but could never quite touch.

"I'd like to hear," she said quietly.

Her brother blushed, then deflected.

"It's easy when there's no competition," he joked lightly. "I was literally the only person there was to speak with for two years."

Self-deprecating humor? His twin was shocked.

"I'm serious," she insisted before continuing on cautiously. "I mean... the two of you were in chains and cages. It's not the easiest way to fall in love."

The room fell quiet as the others looked at them curiously. Only Cassiel seemed to think that chains and cages were still the way to go. The couple shared a swift look before Serafina's face warmed with a heartbreaking kind of smile.

"He broke his arm," she said softly. "Ripped it out of the socket—just to get a few inches closer so he could touch my hand. When Alwyn found us, he..."

She trailed off, overcome with emotion. Kailas reached over freely now to take her hand.

"It was worth it," he said quietly. "I don't care what he did. It was worth every second."

The room was dead quiet. Katerina was holding her breath. Aidan had looked up from his goblet of blood. Even Dylan was staring at the couple with some uncertain emotion.

Tanya's eyes watered as she slipped off of the throne, landing by Katerina's side.

"That's... incredibly romantic."

Yes. Yes, it was.

"It's disgusting," Cassiel replied coldly. "The man ripped his own arm out of the socket."

The shape-shifter flashed him a sour look. "You wouldn't have done it for me?"

His face softened into a charming smile. "Darling, I would never have let myself get chained in the first place."

Kailas opened his mouth to say something, then bowed his head and let it go. Cassiel was the only family Serafina had left, and Kailas was determined to win him over.

No matter how disapproving the fae might be.

"What about you?" he asked instead, steering the conversation to safer ground. "You and Tanya are a charming couple. When did you know that she was the one?"

Cassiel looked up with a start, the crown prince hardly ever addressed him directly. At first, it looked like he was going to ignore the question. Then he found himself actually considering.

"In Laurelwood," he finally replied, staring at his girlfriend as he thought back. "Before that... I didn't realize how much I *didn't* want to kill you until that day."

Aidan pursed his lips, while Katerina looked down with a smile. In his own way, it was probably the most romantic thing Cassiel had ever said.

Although it was by no means the most romantic thing he'd ever done...

"What exactly did it mean?" As the others started talking amongst themselves she sidled up to Serafina, speaking softly under her breath. "What Cass did for Tanya up on the roof?"

She remembered like it was yesterday. The way the fae had cried out as his girlfriend bled to death in his arms. The way he'd murmured under his breath, calling down the light of some distant star. The way that light had travelled from one to the other, opening Tanya's beautiful eyes.

She'd never asked about it. In a way, she didn't feel like it was her place. But now that they were all together, she couldn't hold it in any longer. And his sister was the perfect person to ask.

"Does it mean he's no longer immortal?"

"Not exactly," Serafina answered slowly, gazing thoughtfully at her brother. "It's more like the connection between you and Aidan. He gave a part of himself to her. She'll always have it."

By now, the others were tuning in. Eavesdropping while pretending not to.

"So why don't you just tell your council about the connection?" Katerina asked, turning from one to the other. "If they knew about it, surely they wouldn't try to make you—"

"To do such a thing for an outsider is forbidden by our kind," Cassiel replied softly. "The council would not forgive it."

Tanya shot him a quick look, but said nothing. Katerina, however, pressed onward.

"Yeah, but it's done already. There's nothing they can do. Why wouldn't you just—"

"They *would not* forgive it."

One look at Cassiel's face ended the discussion, and the queen bowed her head with a quiet sigh. A moment later Dylan sat down beside her, gently taking her hand.

"Cass may be one of the last High Born, but you have to remember, in the grand scheme of things he's still very young. He can't just start—"

"That's ridiculous," Katerina interrupted, unable to see him in such a light. "He's *so* old!"

"*Hey.*" Cassiel looked over sharply. "Words are weapons, too, Your Majesty."

Dylan angled between them with a patient smile. "He's not old to the fae. He's just a little over a hundred years old—"

"Closer to five hundred, actually," the fae muttered quietly.

Dylan's mouth fell open in shock, but for one of the first times Cassiel was unable to meet his eyes. He kept his eyes carefully on the floor, fiddling with the edge of his cloak.

"...what?"

Silence.

"I don't understand; you told me—"

"I lied." Cassiel gave him a tentative glance, looking as close to apologetic as Katerina had ever seen him. "You were a teenager when we met, Dylan. Fresh off a traumatic sexual encounter with a Carpathian queen. You asked me how old I was, I didn't want to freak you out... so I lied."

The rest of the group watched with great amusement, but Dylan had never felt so betrayed.

"You... I can't believe that!" he exclaimed. "You just..."

Cassiel raised his eyebrows slowly. "You can't believe that I lied?"

All right, Dylan could believe *that*. From Cassiel. But not from his sister.

"What about you?" he demanded, turning to Serafina. "Did you lie to me as well?"

Her lovely face grimaced apologetically.

"...only a bit."

Tanya snorted as Dylan paled in rage.

"What's a bit?"

Serafina stared down into her cup, swishing the contents guiltily. "You were only off by two... maybe three hundred years."

"Unbelievable!"

As the two started arguing, Katerina turned to Aidan with a whispered hush. "How old are *you*?"

He shrugged innocently. "Old enough."

Katerina tugged his sleeve with a grin. "Come on—tell me!"

He gave her a teasing smile. "I'm between Dylan and Cassiel."

She snorted with muffled laughter. "Oh, all right. So somewhere between eighteen and five-hundred- twelve?"

"Yep."

Meanwhile, the argument was still going strong.

"—just don't see how you can live with yourself. Either one of you."

Dylan sank into a chair, looking as though the foundations of his very world were coming apart at the seams. It was for this reason Katerina made a *concerted* effort to hide her laughter.

"In my defense," Serafina continued, "when we met I was hoping to have a sexual encounter of my own." She flashed an impish grin. "I'm eighteen, Dylan. I can't help it if I'm also immortal."

Katerina's stomach tightened as the smile froze on her face, but it was Kailas who sat forward—staring between the two of them in shock.

"Wait a minute... *the two of you*?"

Serafina flushed with guilt, suddenly looking very much like her brother. But for the first time since finding him chained in the dungeon, Dylan shot the prince a sympathetic look.

"Hurts, doesn't it? Family of sociopathic liars."

"Aw—come on," Cassiel coaxed with a teasing grin. "This doesn't change anything between us. I still love you. I'll still be your friend."

But Dylan was past teasing. In fact, he was putting things together for the first time.

"So all those stories you told me," he said slowly. "Laurelwood, the Great War... they weren't just stories. You were there."

The teasing banter fell away, and for a fleeting moment it was suddenly easy to see how old the two siblings really were. They exchanged a quick look. Five centuries of sadness in their eyes.

"Yes," Cassiel replied softly, "we were there."

The room fell quiet. So painfully quiet that Katerina didn't see how they would ever get past it. But then, just as it was getting hard to breathe, her brother shook his head.

"...I still can't get over that the two of you dated."

A burst of much-needed laughter broke through the heavy silence, thawing the tension as the conversation picked up speed once more.

"I told you I dated a ranger," Serafina said innocently. "One of my brother's friends."

Kailas raised his eyebrows, unimpressed with the distinction. "Yeah, but you didn't tell me it was Dylan."

Much to Katerina's surprise, her brother wasn't alone in his frustration. The second Serafina said the words, Dylan himself leaned forward in disbelief.

"Dated?" he repeated incredulously. "Sera, I asked you to *marry* me."

For the second time, a deathly silence fell over the room.

Serafina stared down at her hands; Cassiel lifted his head in shock. And Dylan paled like he would have given his life to erase the last few seconds he'd spoken.

But that was nothing compared to Katerina. The beautiful queen had turned to stone.

He asked her to marry him?

Without a word, she pushed to her feet and swept out of the room.

Right.

Chapter 12

H*e proposed.*
A wave of liquid fire lay waste to a mannequin, just before she knocked down two more with her fists. They popped back up reluctantly, unwilling to get hit again.

He freakin' PROPOSED!

She'd marched straight to the weapons room after hearing the news, before the words had stopped echoing off the walls. Before she had to see the look of horrified pity on the rest of her friends' faces. Before she had to see Dylan or his would-be bride.

Who knows... maybe it was more than that. Maybe they actually tied the knot!

Quickly as she'd left the room, the queen couldn't help but overhear the things that had happened next. They were forever burned into her brain.

The way Cassiel had stared at his best friend in shock. For once, there was no teasing or humor behind it. Nothing but honest surprise.

"You did?" he'd asked.

Dylan couldn't answer. He was still looking like he was about to be sick. It was Serafina who glanced between them, hanging her head with a sigh.

"Right before the raid on the caravan. The one where I..." She trailed off quietly, eyes fixing on the back of Katerina's head. "I can't believe you didn't tell her."

Another mannequin went down. This one didn't pop back up.

I can't believe you didn't tell her. Katerina gritted her teeth as she whirled around with a high kick, toppling a container of arrows as she smashed in a dummy's nose. *Even SHE thinks it's crazy that I didn't know. Just another thing to add to her perfect freakin' list...*

Faster and faster she flew through the room, losing herself in an endless spiral of rage. But no matter how quickly she moved, no matter how hard she pounded out her aggressions, her mind kept playing it back and a dozen little things started clicking into place.

The way Dylan had stared at Serafina when they'd found her in the dungeons, reaching out to touch her like he was lost in some kind of dream. The look on his face when she'd kissed Kailas, when she'd asked him to shift and search for him in the Kreo desert.

"You want me to find your boyfriend?" he'd asked.

It was another strange moment. Another one full of instant regret. But looking back now, it made perfect sense. His *former fiancée* was asking for help with her *boyfriend*.

Doesn't get more awkward than that.

Unless you count that time your girlfriend found out you'd been engaged.

The queen let out a stifled shriek, pouring out all her rage and fury onto one unfortunate target. Her arms dripped with flames as she hit the thing again and again. Plagued with a hundred images she didn't want to see. Images of Dylan and Serafina together. Of his tender smile as he leaned down to kiss her perfect face. Of the way he'd sunk down onto one knee, gazing up at her with those twinkling blue eyes. Asking her to be his very future—

A hand caught Katerina's wrist and she whipped around to see the actual Dylan standing behind her, looking exactly as pale as when she'd left him in the Great Hall.

"Kat, I..."

It took a lot to leave him speechless. She'd only seen it happen a few times. But no matter how hard he tried now, he couldn't think of a way to finish that sentence.

For a full minute, they stared at each other. One, shaken and lost. The other, dripping a pool of crimson fire onto the tile. When he finally did speak, it was the last thing Katerina wanted to hear.

"I thought she was dead."

There was a beat of silence. Then Katerina stepped back in horror. *Seven hells... it's even worse than I thought.*

"What does that mean?" she choked, arms falling limply back to her sides. "You wouldn't have dated me if you'd known? You would have left me to find her, and never fallen in love—"

"No!" He grabbed the tops of her arms, then jerked back when the fire touched his skin. "I would have tried to find her, of course. But I never would have left you. Nothing in the world could have stopped me from falling in love. It was over between me and Sera. Even if it wasn't, it never would have worked after I met you—"

"It sure didn't look over when you found her in the dungeon," Katerina interrupted, folding her arms protectively over her chest. "I've never seen you look like that before. You literally reached out to touch her to make sure she was real—"

"Because I thought she was dead!" he said again, desperate to make her believe him. "Kat, I swear to you, that's the only thing I was thinking—"

"Then why didn't you just tell me?"

A deafening silence rang out between them. Growing louder and louder every second he didn't reply. When it became clear that he couldn't, Katerina took another step away.

"We tell each other everything, Dylan." She gestured between them. "That's the only way this thing works. And considering how many people are trying to tear us apart, you can't just—"

"I had no idea *how* to tell you. I was...I was scared."

It wasn't often he admitted such a thing. It took a lot for him to do so now.

"Katerina, I..." He trailed off, running a hand back through his hair. "It was an impossible situation. I loved Sera very much, enough to make me stupid about it, but I thought she'd been killed almost two years ago. I grieved. I moved on. I met you."

Those blue eyes pierced her, begging her to believe.

"When I found her that day in the dungeon, I felt like the whole world had turned upside-down. Here she was—alive. And very much in love with someone else. And the two of us had never technically broken up, but we clearly weren't together. I just... panicked. I convinced myself it was in the past and it didn't matter, and we should all just move on with a clean slate."

Katerina listened quietly, keeping her eyes on him the whole time. It was a heartfelt speech, that much was sure. But with one or two gaping holes torn through the middle.

"It was in the past?" she repeated incredulously. "It didn't matter?"

"She was with Kailas. I was with you." He tried to reach for her again, but was stopped once more by those dancing flames. "We didn't love each other anymore—"

"You asked her to *marry* you!" Katerina cried. "You loved her enough for *that*!"

"Kat, I swear to you. It wasn't what you think—"

"What? You didn't love her?" she interrupted. "Because that doesn't just disappear!"

He took a deep breath, trying to steady his shaking hands. "Of course I loved her; I was in love with her, I just—"

"Then what?" A part of Katerina was vaguely aware that she wasn't letting him finish a sentence, but a more frightened part didn't want to hear what he had to say. "You asked her to *marry* you, Dylan. What did you want—"

"I wanted a *family*!"

He took a step back, shaking from head to toe.

"I wanted a family, more than I wanted..."

His head fell to his chest, shoulders rising and falling quickly though he could never quite seem to catch his breath. After a few seconds of trying, he gave up and simply pushed through.

"When I met Sera and Cass, I'd just lost everyone I'd ever loved. Parents, siblings, uncles, cousins. My entire family, wiped out all on the same day. I was young. I was lonely. I'd attached desperately to these new friends that I trusted and loved."

He forced himself to lift his head, to look her in the eyes.

"They had each other—bound by blood. And I wanted to be a part of it. I loved Sera. We'd been dating a few months; I thought... that's what marriage is. Loving someone. Having a family."

His words, gentle as they were, tore at Katerina's heart. The quiet honesty ripped through her like a knife. She could imagine it perfectly. The three of them, together. Bound for all eternity.

"But I don't want that with you."

Her head snapped up and her mouth fell open. She was so surprised, those deadly flames vanished clear away. "You don't...you don't want to be my family?"

He closed the distance between them, taking her by the hand. "I want to be your *husband*. I want you to be my *wife*."

Each word was said slowly. Deliberately. Like he'd thought about them for a long time.

"Yes, I want to be your family. I want to build a family with you. But I want something more than that. I want the marriage. I want—"

"But it doesn't matter what you want." She pulled away suddenly, her eyes spilling over with tears. "*Everyone* wants you to be with her. This perfect, beautiful girl you already proposed to. The five kingdoms have managed to unite on a single issue, and it's that you and Serafina should be—"

"I couldn't give a *damn* about the five kingdoms." His eyes flashed, and even though she tried to pull away he held on to her hands. "I told you last night, Katerina, it's *you* and *me*."

She wanted to believe him. She wanted it more than she'd wanted anything in her whole life. But it wasn't that simple. There were other forces at play. And no matter how much he wanted to deny it, no matter how hard he tried to compartmentalize them away, they weren't going anywhere.

"And how exactly would we build a family?" she challenged, all those secret fears bursting forth as her eyes spilled over with tears. "You and Sera would have an immortal shifter. But what about us? What would *we* have?"

"We'd have a wolf."

"We'd have a dragon."

They froze at the same time, then stared at each other in silence.

Never once had he thought about it. Never once had he thought about anything other than a life of blissful happiness with the girl standing in front of him.

Katerina had thought about it the moment she transformed for the first time.

"Then..." Dylan's mind raced as he struggled to find the right words. "Then we just won't have a child. I don't need a child, Kat. I only need you."

He was speaking now without thinking. The way he did when he was desperate.

The way he did when he was wrong.

"You're the king of Belaria, I'm the queen of the High Kingdom," she said quietly, tears still streaming down her face. "We're asking people to let us join all that together. And now you're saying that neither kingdom will have an heir?"

"I don't need Belaria," he said fiercely, tearing apart his life one thing after the other. "The only reason I went back was for you. If you wanted, I'd give it all up. So could you. We could run away together, just the two of us—"

"That's ridiculous; *listen* to what you're saying!" she cried. "We only started this conversation because you failed to tell me you'd asked another woman to *marry* you, and now you're saying that we should give up our kingdoms and the chance to have kids, and run off into the woods—"

"There's no alternative," he said softly. "Not for me. If that's the only way to be together..."

She tried to pull away, but he held tight to her hands.

"Kat, I told you once that we don't get to choose our stars. I was wrong. We *do* get to choose them, and I choose you. I want you. I *love* you... more than anything in this world." His eyes shone with desperate sincerity as they stared down into hers. "Give me a thousand years, and I'd never stop loving you. I've never felt that way before. I'll never feel it again. You're it for me."

She could feel his heartbeat in his hands. The strong pulse as he held them together. She took a step closer. She wanted to believe...

Then reality set in and she took a step away.

"I don't know if that's enough."

KATERINA DIDN'T REMEMBER walking back to her room. Her feet moved robotically, one step after another, trudging back up the winding stairs. She supposed a lot of people saw her. All those people she and Dylan had been hiding from just an hour before. In hindsight, a lot of them moved to stop her, to try to engage, but they all stopped cold at the look on her face.

Thus, she proceeded back to her bedroom. Silently crying. Lost in thought.

How is it possible that things were easier when we were living in the woods? On the run from the royal army? An impossible bounty on our heads?

One foot after the other. Step after step.

I believed the two of us would have a future—even when it was more likely that both of us were going to end up dead. Now that we're finally home safe... I don't know if we can even spend that future together.

She pulled open the door without thinking, prepared to fling herself miserably onto the bed, then just about had a heart attack when a quiet voice called to her from the balcony.

"Katerina?"

The queen jumped back with a gasp, hand clutched over her chest. For a second, there was no one with her. Then Serafina walked hesitantly into the room.

Really? Now?

She truly was breathtaking. There was no other word to describe it.

Tall, slender body. Glowing porcelain skin. The kind of delicate features you imagined on things like angels, with a pair of enormous onyx eyes that seemed to take up half of her face. All that framed by billowing curtains of ivory hair.

She was exquisite. A true princess of the Fae. But there was steel beneath the honey. A legend behind the doll. This was the kind of girl Katerina had wanted to be when she grew up. A girl who would have been just as comfortable sitting on the edge of a cloud as riding a war horse into battle. As fierce as she was beautiful. As respected as she was loved.

I probably DID want to be her when I grew up. It was probably her ACUTAL picture in my books.

"Hi, Sera." The young queen fidgeted uncomfortably, trying to think of something normal to say. She gave up a second later. "You know what, could you just go and be perfect elsewhere?"

The fae froze a moment, thrown by the unexpected honesty, than perched on the edge of the bed with a little smile. "I'd be happy to... if you'd talk with me a moment first?"

Katerina gritted her teeth and stifled a sigh. She forgotten, when listing her rival's unending attributes she was also infuriatingly stubborn. A daughter of the Fae, through and through.

"The thing is, now's not really the best time—"

"I said no," Serafina interrupted softly. "Did he tell you that?"

Katerina stopped short, looking down at her in surprise. No, Dylan had most certainly *not* told her that. Not that she'd let him finish many of his sentences. In no wretched version she'd been imagining over the last hour had she possibly considered the fact that Serafina would say no.

"You did?" she asked incredulously, sinking down without thinking onto the bed. "Why?"

"Because he didn't really want to marry me!" Serafina laughed. "And I didn't want to marry him. We were *dating*, he and I. It wasn't that kind of love."

Katerina blinked back at her, at a complete loss as to what to say.

"Sweet girl," the fae leaned forward, taking her gently by the hand, "he asked me because he was young. He was impulsive. I mean, you should have seen some of the things that he—" Katerina flinched and she caught herself quickly. "You're right, not helping."

It was quiet for a moment, before the fae tried again.

"My point is... it wasn't real."

Their eyes locked.

"Not like what I have with Kailas. Not like what you have with him."

It was quiet for a moment. A *long* moment. Then Katerina shook her head.

"I just don't understand why he wouldn't tell me—"

She stopped short when Serafina started laughing. An infectious tinkling sound that left a warm afterglow in its wake. "Do you remember what I told you that night in the desert? How I'd never seen Dylan look at anyone the way he was looking at you?"

Katerina nodded, and the fae flashed a knowing smile.

"I've been around a long time, Katerina. A fact I've only recently been forced to admit. So believe me when I tell you that love like that doesn't come around very often. It's a rare thing, what the two of you have. It should be cherished, not questioned. You should thank your lucky stars."

The queen looked up suddenly as an echo of Dylan's voice floated through her mind.

You get to choose your stars. And I choose you.

"But how can such a thing ever last?" she asked quietly. "Literally the *entire world* is standing against us. We have responsibilities. A whole realm of people who depend on us to act with *their* best interests at heart. How do you just *will* problems like that away?"

Serafina laughed again, and in spite of her best intentions Katerina began to smile.

"You think you have problems?" the fae asked. "You and Dylan are both mortal. You can have a future together, live out your lives standing side by side. What about me and Kailas? An immortal princess with a mortal prince? At least your problems have an expiration date, Kat."

It was truly one of the strangest conversations she'd ever had. Certainly not something to laugh about. And yet, that's exactly what Katerina found herself doing just a moment later.

"I'm sorry," she gasped, wiping her eyes as the stress and shock of the day slowly melted off her shoulders. "It's not funny, I just—"

"You have to laugh," Serafina said quickly. "We all do. There's only so much we can control before the rest is out of our hands. But I do know this," she continued as they quieted down. "Love brings people together for a reason. And the fates are not intentionally cruel."

She squeezed Katerina's hand, offering her a hopeful smile.

"These things have a way of working themselves out."

If you'd told Katerina an hour before that she and Serafina would be laughing together in her room, talking about true love and the future, she would have thrown you off the northern tower.

But here they were all the same. A queen of men, and a princess of the Fae.

Finally seeing eye to eye.

"You know, if I'm being honest, it's actually kind of sweet." Katerina kicked up her feet on the mattress, leaning against the headboard. "That Dylan wanted so badly to make you and Cass his family. He told me once that, when he was little, he wanted to grow up and become Fae."

Serafina grinned, reclining on the cushion beside her. "I imagine that didn't go over so well with the Belarian Council..."

"His father threw a fit," Katerina laughed again. "Told him he wasn't showing the proper pride. Said that a true shifter of Belaria would never trade blood with a fae."

"*Trade blood*," Serafina snorted, rolling her eyes. "That sounds like Aldrich. The Hales were all such monsters, it's amazing that someone like Dylan came from people like them."

Katerina shook her head with a smile, staring up at the ceiling.

"It must have been his little dream. Growing up with you and Cass in Taviel. Trying to win his own magical bird—"

She jerked upright with a gasp, Serafina's hand wrapped around her wrist. For a moment the fae just stared at her, those enormous eyes clouding over with memories of days long since passed.

Then her lips parted with a single, whispered word.

"*Taviel.*"

The next second, she was pulling Katerina to her feet. That lovely face pale with dread.

"We need to speak with my brother..."

Chapter 13

" ... W ould you just slow down a minute? I'm not even wearing shoes..."

The queen and the fae raced up one hall and down another. Darting around corners. Tearing through doorways. Leaping over balconies. Not bothering with little details like breathing and stairs.

"...think you dislocated my wrist, by the way..."

A pair of shifters stumbled backwards to avoid getting run over. They let loose a slew of dirty oaths, then they saw who they were shouting at and quickly bowed their heads with respect.

"...so not what I meant when I said we should be friends..."

Katerina might as well have been talking to a wall. From the moment the fateful word *Taviel* passed her lips, the fae had lost all sense of the world around her. She'd leapt to her feet and flown out the door in a blur of hair and silk, pausing only long enough to drag the queen along with her.

They'd been flat-out sprinting ever since, dashing through the castle, and she'd yet to do anything but mutter incoherently to herself. Speaking in quiet, stilted sentences.

"Can't believe I didn't put it together before." They raced beneath a portrait of the late queen, smiling tranquilly down on their manic flight. "But it *has* been over four hundred years..."

Another towering stairwell and Katerina pulled desperately on her captive arm, feeling as though both legs were about to fall off. "Seven hells, woman! Stop! I can't do this—"

One slammed into the other as they came to a screeching halt.

"—anymore."

They were in the upper levels of the castle now, where only royalty and the highest-ranking delegates were permitted to sleep. Katerina

146

pulled in a broken gasp, staring at the tall arched door that led to Cassiel's chamber. His sister was frozen by her side, barely out of breath.

"Sera, hold on a second." Katerina could feel the waves of manic energy rolling off the fae, and the girl must have mentally checked out in the east wing if she didn't recognize the sounds coming from the other side of her brother's door. The breathless moans and creaking mattress could mean only one thing. "Just take a breath, tell me what—"

"Need to talk to Cass..." Serafina interrupted quietly, reaching past her to knock frantically on the door. "He'll know what to do."

Katerina stepped back with a grimace, already bracing for the disaster to come.

She had accidentally interrupted Cassiel and Tanya just once before, after returning from an impromptu transformation to find that her window had been locked. To complete her humiliation she'd alighted clumsily on their windowsill, only to find that her friends had also misplaced their clothes and were far too preoccupied to notice the blushing girl tapping on the glass.

The shape-shifter had thought the entire thing was hilarious. The fae had frozen a moment in surprise before graciously inviting her to join them.

Needless to say, it was an experience she didn't care to repeat.

"Sera, seriously—I'm sure it can wait."

But waiting wasn't something little sisters did for their older brothers. No matter how indisposed that older brother might happen to be. The knocking increased. Tenfold.

Here we go again...

At first, the couple seemed determined to ignore them. If anything, the volume increased. It was the world's most uncomfortable stand-off, but when their persistent visitor showed no signs of abating the room fell abruptly quiet—then echoed with an unmistakable curse.

There was a soft rustling of sheets. The telltale creaking of floorboards as a pair of light footsteps headed their way. A second later the door pulled open to reveal a breathtaking, sex-tousled prince.

A look of pure murder in his eyes.

"Go away."

There wasn't an ounce of humor in his face as he bypassed Katerina entirely and glared down at his sister—the perpetrator of this little crime. An ivory robe with gold stitching had been pulled hastily over his shoulders, and there were incriminating tangles throughout his silken hair.

Ignoring him entirely, Serafina took a fearless step closer.

"Cass—"

His eyes flashed as his hand tightened threateningly on the door.

While he was usually quite indulgent with his little sister, he had no time for her now. His mind was obviously on other things. Things that were waiting back in his bed.

"*Maleos.*"

It was a word Katerina wasn't exactly familiar with, but had come to understand meant something very bad in the language of the fae.

"I will strangle you with my bare hands. Leave."

He certainly looked quite ready to deliver on the threat, but his little sister wasn't exactly the type to flinch. Instead, she pushed straight past him into the room, ignoring the scandalized yelp as Tanya hurried to pull the blankets up around her chest.

"Sera!" Cassiel thundered.

"Kat?" Tanya echoed.

"This was *not* my idea!" Katerina hastened to reply.

"QUIET!" Serafina shouted. The rest of the room seemed to fall away as her eyes locked with impossible intensity on her brother. "I need to speak with you."

There was a moment of silence, then Tanya turned to her boyfriend.

"You said she'd grow on me. She is *not* growing on me."

Under normal circumstances, Cassiel would have hurried to console her. But the second he heard his sister shout, his body had frozen very still. The siblings locked eyes, and if she didn't know better Katerina could have sworn they were reading each other's thoughts.

"What is it?" he asked softly. "What's happened?"

Serafina didn't bother with a context. She jumped right in.

"Taviel."

Cassiel's whole body seemed to flinch, while Tanya rolled her eyes with a sarcastic undertone. "Crap, she guessed our safe word."

"Kerien was trying to tell us something," Serafina repeated earnestly. *"Taviel."*

A look of genuine hurt flashed across Cassiel's face, as if the word itself caused him physical pain. "Sera, we've been through this—"

"Not the city," she insisted. "The *forest.*"

A heavy silence descended upon the room, and without even knowing what they were talking about Katerina's stomach tightened with a sudden sense of dread. She and Tanya were staring back and forth in complete bewilderment, but the fae only had eyes for each other. And whatever it was they were talking about... clearly wasn't good.

"What was that story you told me?" Serafina asked quietly. "The one about the children who went hiking in the woods. What did you say happened to them?"

Katerina turned back to Cassiel, but the fae was beyond the point of speech. His face had turned a deathly shade of pale, and without seeming to think about it he started shaking his head.

"No...no, that isn't possible..."

Tanya got slowly to her feet, clutching the blanket around her. "Babe?"

"I..." He took a step back, eyes wide with fear. "I don't..."

"What happened to the hikers, brother?" Serafina's gaze burned intently into his. "How did the story end?"

A tremble shook through the fearless warrior before he went suddenly still.

"They fell blind."

Three simple words, but they changed everything. Three simple words, but Katerina instinctively knew her world was never going to be the same.

"Cass...?"

Tanya had seen her boyfriend take down monsters and demons. She'd seen him stare death in the face and charge headlong into battle. But never once had she seen him afraid. Until now.

"Cass, what does that mean?"

There was a moment of silence. Then everything started to unravel.

"Get dressed, love." Cassiel's dark eyes locked on the door. "And hurry."

THERE IS NOTHING MORE terrifying than watching one of the strongest people you know fall apart at the seams. It's as if the very ground you're standing on starts to quake.

Cassiel tried not to show it. He was damn convincing, too. To anyone watching from the outside, there was nothing at all unusual in the way he swept gracefully down the long corridor. Not a single hint to clue them in on his enchanting face. But there was something in the quickness of his step that made Katerina tremble. A flicker of panic in his eyes that made her skin run cold.

"Where are we going?" she whispered to Tanya.

In times of crisis, the fae locked down. Try as they might to get any information, the siblings had no intention of sharing just yet. Instead, the queen and the shape-shifter were following a few paces behind, struggling a bit to keep up with their long strides.

"No idea." Tanya had been so surprised by her boyfriend's sudden change of heart that she hadn't even argued against it. She simply did as he asked, dressing quickly before following him out into the hall. "Sera didn't say anything when you guys were talking? Which is *weird*, by the way."

"What—that we were talking?"

Tanya flashed her a quick look, the tension and nerves prompting an ill-timed joke.

"Unless you were comparing notes? Sharing wedding ideas? Two brides, one groom?"

In the wake of their sudden departure, Katerina had actually forgotten. The revelation that had brought the two girls together in the first place. The strange reconciliation while laughing together on the bed. The tips of her fingers began to smoke, and Tanya backed off with a faint grin.

"...or not." The fae picked up the pace and that grin faded into a worried frown. "But seriously," she lowered her voice, "Sera didn't say anything?"

Katerina shook her head. Everything the fae *had* said, she'd muttered to herself. And most of it had been in a language Katerina couldn't understand. Something about that fateful word had the siblings worried. Terrified, in fact. But that was all she knew for sure.

Trying hard to contain her panic, she shot Tanya a sideways glance.

"Sorry we burst in on you guys."

The shape-shifter shook her head. "Don't be—it was weird anyway." She flashed a glance at the back of Cassiel's head. "I felt like that bird was watching me..."

That was the last thing either of them said until they'd made their way back down to the ground floor. It was only then that Katerina realized she might want to send a servant to contact her *own* boyfriend, let him know what was happening. But no sooner had she thought his name, than Dylan and Kailas suddenly emerged from one of the studies in the Great Hall, walking side by side.

What the heck is this?

For a moment, the sight of them standing together was enough to stop even Cassiel in his tracks. Both groups froze at the same time, staring awkwardly, searching for something to say.

Comb through the five kingdoms and you'd be hard pressed to find a less likely pair. The leader of the rebellions and a prince whose sins stopped just shy of genocide. And yet, here they were. Frozen with the same guilty flush. Staring at the one point of commonality between them. A living, breathing white flag. The bewildered girl with the smoking hands.

Katerina took a tentative step, half-expecting to see a knife sticking out of both their backs.

"Hey, what are you—"

But there was no time.

Before anyone could explain, Cassiel grabbed the ranger by the sleeve and started dragging him along—speaking in such a fast clip Katerina could scarcely understand.

Random words jumped out at her. Things like *Taviel. Kerien.* And something else, too; a word she'd learned back in Laurelwood all those months ago. The fae word for 'curse.'

"Wait—what?"

Dylan pulled against Cassiel's vise-like grasp, trying to make sense of the barrage of things the fae was throwing at him. He tried to interject a question, speaking in his friend's native tongue, feet slipping a bit against the slick stone. By the time he tried again, they came to a sudden stop.

"Are you sure about this?" His eyes tightened with worry as he glanced between Cassiel and the door. "If you're wrong—"

Cassiel didn't answer. He simply raised his hand and knocked.

The sound rang out in the hallway, drawing curious looks from the scattered people passing by. It was only then that Katerina realized where they were. Why it was that people were staring.

They were pounding on the door to the morgue.

Oh... this can't be good.

The castle didn't used to have a morgue, the same way it didn't used to have a chapel. Then her father decided to wage war with the five kingdoms, and people decided they needed a place to put their dead and to pray. Katerina remembered the day the first body was carried inside. She and Kailas had watched from the stairwell, trying to recall what the room had been used for before.

To this day, she still couldn't remember.

"What do you want?"

The door pulled open and a tiny man stepped outside. Thick beard, heavy armor, and the perpetual scowl she'd come to associate with dwarves. He was immediately flanked by two others.

"Speak," he demanded. There was a pile of personal effects on the floor beside him, and he seemed less than thrilled with the choice of visitors. "Why have you come here?"

At this point, Dylan stepped forward quickly. He might have grasped only half of what was going on, but there was a long-standing grudge between the dwarves and Fae. Of this he was sure.

"We're sorry to disturb you," he began in a placating voice he rarely used, "especially at a time such as this. But we were hoping you might—"

"Was your friend blind?" Cassiel interrupted, pushing to the foreground. When the dwarves stared at him in shock, he callously clarified, "The dead one."

Katerina's hand drifted to her mouth as Dylan's eyes snapped shut with a grimace.

"Seven hells," he murmured. "You're going to get us all killed."

The dwarf who'd pushed open the door stormed forward, until they were standing toe to toe. While he might have only come up to the fae's waist, he was by no means intimidated. Quite the contrary, his fingers twitched with anticipation, as if he was aching to reach for his axe.

"Say that again," he growled, staring up with the blackest hate. "Say it one more time."

Dylan and Tanya tensed at the same time, hands drifting to their sides though both were surprisingly without a blade. The dwarves planted their feet firmly, ready for anything.

Only one man remained immune to the tension. The same man who'd ironically caused it.

"I have no time for your anger or your offense," Cassiel replied impatiently, glancing over their bushy heads as if hoping to see for himself. "Your friend... was he blind?"

The dwarf bristled with unspeakable anger, and for a second Katerina thought he might take a swing at the fae right then and there. Those thick bands of muscles tensed and coiled, straining the leather stitching on his sleeves.

"It isn't enough that you people killed him, now you come here asking questions?!" he roared. "What does it matter if he was blind, the man's DEAD!"

"*You people?*" Serafina swept forward, as lethal as she was lovely. "Your friend was not killed by the fae. In case you'd forgotten, we lost one of our own as well."

The dwarf shot her a glare, but kept his rage focused on her brother. Serafina was a bit of a conundrum to his people. While the dwarves might have vowed to despise the Fae until the end of time, it was hard to look at their angel-faced princess with that same kind of hate.

"No one believes their deaths were caused by witches," he snarled. "We've conducted our own investigation to determine blame."

"Who else is on the shortlist?" Dylan muttered.

In hindsight, it was an unfortunate choice of words.

His eyes flashed up with apology as the dwarf in charge turned to him with a savage glare.

"I didn't mean—"

There was a sickening crunch as the dwarf punched him right in the stomach, doubling him over with a gasp of pain. But instead of straightening up the way Katerina had seen him do a million times before, he stayed down. A second later, he fell to his knees.

"We buried Lokni this morning," the dwarf growled, rubbing his knuckles as he fixed Cassiel with another glare. "And even if we'd checked his eyes, I have no interest in helping you. Be gone from this place, and may a curse be on all your heads."

The door slammed shut. Leaving a ringing silence in its wake.

That went well.

"Dylan!" Katerina gasped, darting forward. She helped the ranger shakily to his feet, truly astonished by the force of the blow. "Are you all right?"

"Yeah," he muttered, clutching gingerly at the base of his ribs. "Cass, I don't—"

"We need to dig him up."

The others froze in disbelief. Some frightened, some bewildered, all of them too stunned to speak. Katerina recovered herself first. If only partially.

"Dig him up?" she repeated slowly. "As in... dig up the dwarf's body?"

"Cassiel, *listen* to me." Dylan took his friend by the shoulder. Half to restrain, half because he was still unable to stand. "To do that is to risk *actual war* with the dwarves. It isn't a decision we're going to make in this hallway. It isn't a decision we're going to make at all—"

But the fae's mind was already made up. And nothing in the world was going to change it.

"Get the vampire. We'll meet in the woods."

THE SUN WAS ALREADY beginning to dip lower in the sky when Katerina split off from the rest of the group and headed up the stairs to get Aidan. Kailas was going to go with her, but he was unwilling to leave his girlfriend. Tanya was going to go with her, but she was unwilling to leave her boyfriend. Dylan was going to go with her, but he was afraid of what Cassiel might do if left alone.

In the end, she was on her own. Off to make one of the strangest requests of her life.

Just relax. You've done weirder things than this. So has he.

She pulled in a deep breath, paused, then knocked softly on Aidan's door. Half-hoping he wouldn't answer. Half-desperate that he would.

There was no progression of sounds when it came to a vampire. No footsteps, or breathing, or creaking floorboards to track one's progress. One second, she was standing alone at the door. The next, Aidan was pulling it open. Vampires were swift as shadows. There was no in between.

"Hey." He leaned against the frame with a charming smile, looking uncharacteristically relaxed with messy hair and bare feet. "I was just about to..." That smile faded when he saw the look on her face. "Kat... what did you do?"

"*I* didn't do anything," she said quickly, thrilled that for once it was true. "But the others were wondering if you'd come out to the woods and... help with a little favor."

It wasn't wise to play games with a vampire, and Aidan was better than most. His dark eyes narrowed as they looked Katerina up and down. Always seeing the girl, never seeing the crown.

"And what, pray tell, might this little favor be?"

She bit her lower lip, stalling.

"Actually," she said with a stroke of brilliance, "it's one of those things that's kind of better as a surprise—"

In a flash, he was standing right in front of her. Staring down with a hint of a smile in those dark, eternal eyes. She sucked in a silent breath, flushed with guilt as he cocked his head to the side.

"What is it? Just tell me." She froze, like a mouse before a snake, and he laughed softly. "I can feel your panic attack from here. Just say it, Katerina. It can't be that bad."

Yes...yes, it can.

She pulled in a deep breath, panicked and decided to leave, got dragged back, then finally exhaled it all in a single breath. "We're exhuming the body of that dwarf to see if he was blind like the fae, because Cass and Sera think there's some weird curse that has something to do with Taviel."

Actually, he was right. I do feel a lot better getting that off my chest.

Aidan blinked. Parted his lips to say something. Then blinked again.

On second thought, maybe I should have kept it to myself after all.

It wasn't easy to surprise a vampire. Most of them had been around long enough to have already seen just about anything you could throw their way. Under different circumstances, Katerina might have been proud to do it now. As it was, she just stood there, fidgeting nervously, feeling the waves of shock roll off of him like an intemperate tide.

"You want me to help you dig up a grave."

He didn't phrase it as a question, yet there was nothing but utter disbelief in his eyes. The queen cast a quick glance behind her before closing the gap between them.

"To be honest," she lowered her voice conspiratorially, "I'd have thought you'd have some experience with things like this."

Aidan's eyebrows lifted ever so slightly. The same way they did when she'd walked him past a mirror in the portrait hall, sneaking a sideways look to see if he had a reflection.

"You think I have experience digging up graves." Again, not a question. "Because, like the rest of the undead, I'm just tickled pink by the whole idea of corpses."

The queen started to get the feeling that he wasn't quite being sincere.

"I don't want to do it, either," she said quickly, "but the whole gang is out there—"

"And you thought to include me?" He lifted a sentimental hand to his chest, eyes narrowing with a caustic glare. "Thank you, Katerina. What a lovely group activity."

He backed into his room before she could stop him, swinging the door shut. She was only barely able to catch it in time, wedging her foot in the frame.

"Aidan—"

"Do me a favor, princess," he had attended her coronation like everyone else, but to him it had always been more of a nickname than a title, "next time you decide to go digging up bodies in the woods, come and get me *afterwards*. Or, better yet, just tell me about it the next day."

He banged the door lightly against her foot, and she folded her arms with a glare.

"Look, this wasn't my idea. You think *I* want to go unearthing corpses in the middle of the woods? Cassiel won't take no for an answer—"

"Wait... this was *Cassiel's* idea?"

Occasional bursts of whimsy aside, Cassiel could generally be counted on to be more level-headed than the rest of the gang. To have him suggest such a thing was enough to make Aidan re-open the door with a look of genuine surprise.

"It was a little scary," Katerina admitted in a soft undertone. "The second Serafina came to him with this story, he just... freaked out." A shiver ran through her as she recalled the look of fear on the fae's face. The quiet terror that settled in his eyes. "I've never seen him like that before."

Aidan's face tightened as he stared down at her. Feeling her fear as if it was his own. Reliving the panic as if he'd experienced it as well. The blood connection made him highly attuned to such things, but the rest was just Aidan. He could sense these things long before they'd shared blood.

For a moment, his dark eyes lost themselves in the space over her head. Clouding with a heavy layer of worry. Then he glanced back down at Katerina and bowed his head with a quiet sigh.

"Just give me a minute."

He made to shut the door again, but Katerina caught it quickly in her hand.

"Promise me you're not going to just jump out the window or something."

He stared at her a moment before the corner of his mouth twitched up in a little grin.

"We're digging up a grave... I need to put on some shoes."

Chapter 14

It didn't matter who wanted to speak with you, or what kind of trouble you were in... *everyone* left you alone when you were walking with a vampire.

Katerina stayed close beside Aidan as they made their way out of the castle, watching the chain reaction with the hint of a grin. Since publicly announcing she was obliged to marry her boyfriend's best friend, it seemed there was no shortage of dignitaries and nobles who urgently wished to speak with her. Some of the most powerful men in the five kingdoms, but one by one they melted away. Atticus Gail, Leonor, Abel Bishop. Even Hastings, her beloved guard, was hesitant to approach with Aidan standing by her side. She watched them all awkwardly changing direction. Walking back into rooms from which they'd just emerged. Acting as though they hadn't seen her in the first place. Anything to avoid such close proximity to the vampire.

It was like he was invisible while being the very opposite at the same time. Deliberately unseen specifically because of the weight of his presence. Rather than shying away from it, Aidan took constant advantage of such anonymity. Retaining his privacy any chance he got.

But, like most things, Katerina wondered if it wouldn't have been his choice. If he would have traded some of that coveted isolation for just a few hours of being seen.

"Are you smiling?"

His sharp voice cut through the reverie and she hastened to hide her grin. A pair of passing shifters looked at them curiously as she forced her face into a thoughtful frown.

"Of course not," she scoffed, as if he'd asked a very stupid question. "Why would I be—"

"Because we're about to unearth a body."

"I know that—"

"A task I wish *very much* you'd left me out of."

"I'm not smiling, Aidan," she said quickly. It was quiet for a moment before she flashed him a sideways grin. "...but I'm happy you're here."

The two stepped out of the castle the very moment the sun kissed the horizon, sending up a blinding array of burnt golds and rusted crimson in its wake. The double doors swung shut with a resounding *clang* behind them and the voices inside vanished with a sudden hush.

"They just said to meet in the woods," Katerina began uncertainly, eyes scanning the endless tree line, "I'm not sure where exactly they meant..."

Aidan glanced around, then pulled them to a sudden stop in the middle of the walkway. As she looked on curiously he closed his eyes and lifted his chin ever so slightly, almost as if he was sniffing the breeze. His body stilled in absolute focus, and she found herself holding her breath.

Dylan, she realized in wonder. *He can sense Dylan.*

His eyes snapped open, zeroing in on a specific spot in the trees before he strode briskly across the grass, pulling Katerina along with him. "Not a word to the ranger."

She bit back a smile, trying to imagine the look on her boyfriend's face if he realized exactly how well the vampire was able to keep tabs on him.

"What about me?" she asked instead. "It must be a hundred times easier with me."

Unlike Dylan, who'd never tasted the vampire's blood, her connection went both ways.

"You'd think so, but it's actually quite hard." He flashed her a little smile. "You're a dragon, Katerina. Dragons never stay in the same place too long."

The two carried on in silence until they made it all the way to the trees. No one came running out from the castle to stop them. No contingent of armored dwarves sprang up in their path. For the first time since Cassiel announced his dreadful plan, Katerina thought they might actually have a chance of getting away with it.

It wasn't long before they heard movement through the trees. They were able to pick out individual voices not long after that. At least, it took Katerina a moment; it had probably been easier for her buddy walking beside her.

"What do you mean, you didn't bring a shovel?" Dylan was demanding. "Cass, that's like showing up to a dinner party with no wine. *You* were the one who wanted to do this—"

"I assumed you would shift," the fae answered stiffly.

"Shift?!"

"Dylan, that's not a bad idea," Serafina interjected softly.

He ignored her, glaring at the fae just as Aidan and Katerina walked out of the trees. "First you ask me to help you dig up a body, then you insist I do it naked? Oh—hey, babe."

Katerina slipped her hand into his as Cassiel threw an impatient glance at the setting sun.

"Dylan, it's hardly the first time I've asked you to dig up a body."

Aidan leaned back against a tree with a sigh. "So happy you called me out here for this..."

"Guys!" Tanya came bounding into the clearing, holding something in her hand. "I found the shovel they used to bury him in the first place."

She tossed it to Katerina, who tossed it to Dylan, who threw it abruptly into Kailas' face.

"I think the prince should do it," Dylan announced. "Find out just how much those muscles atrophied when you were wasting away in chains."

Katerina pulled back her hand with a gasp, but to her extreme surprise her brother flashed a playful grin, catching the shovel an inch away from his face.

"Never send a dog to do a man's work..." He hopped into the grave without another word, moving with a strength and speed to match any of the men standing around him.

After only a minute or two Dylan leapt down and joined him, alternating turns with the shovel. Before long, there was a small mountain of dirt on the forest floor.

Katerina had a hundred questions. Not the least of which was whether they were going to end up with two new bodies to add to the grave. But, despite the odd display of teamwork, her eyes were drawn somewhere else. To the Fae prince watching their every move.

Since the moment she'd met him, Katerina had always thought of Cassiel as dignified. Regal. More refined than the others. Between that and his starlit features, she hadn't been at all surprised to discover he was a prince. Now, looking at him in the presence of his people, it was easy to see how different he'd become. Unlike the rest of his kind, he hadn't shut himself away from the outside world. He'd embraced it as best he could. Modernizing. Changing with the times. Adapting to an extent that would have scandalized the older members of his people.

In the eyes of the Fae, he'd grown rather wild. But the prince still remained. As dignified as the day they'd met. And never once, not for a single moment, had Katerina seen him lose control.

Until today.

The man in front of her wasn't in control. He looked... stricken. Manic eyes followed every motion of the shovel. Hands twitched with anticipation. Hanging on by the most delicate thread.

"We found something."

Kailas stopped digging at once as Dylan sank slowly to his knees. Half-hoping they were wrong, that there was nothing in the hole but freshly turned dirt, he felt around carefully until his hands came upon something hard. There was a hitch in his breathing. His entire body froze with dread. Then slowly, carefully, he pulled a small shrouded figure from the ground.

Even though she'd been expecting it, the sight was still a shock. Katerina let out a silent gasp, taking an automatic step away from the scene. Tanya and Serafina both looked decidedly grim and Aidan peeled himself slowly off the tree, watching with sharp, attentive eyes.

"Cass, are you sure?" There was something to be said for how far they'd already come but, holding the body of the dwarf in his arms, Dylan seemed unable to pull back the shroud. "I can't—"

"Stand aside."

Cassiel leapt gracefully into the grave, seizing the body for himself. His fingers unwrapped the shroud with the practiced speed of one who'd shrouded many bodies before, and before they knew it the angry dwarf from the banquet hall was lying before their eyes.

"I can't..." Tanya backed away, looking green. "I'm going to be sick."

The others were frozen with similar expressions. It was one thing to disturb a grave. It was quite another to be holding the corpse in your arms.

Cassiel stared down without emotion. Seeing the dwarf without seeing him, all at the same time. He pulled in a silent breath then, with surprisingly delicate fingers, lifted back the eyelids.

Katerina half-expected him to come alive. For him to leap out of the ground with a shout and hack them all to pieces with his beloved axe. But the dwarf did none of those things. He lay quiet and still in the fae's arms, almost like a sleeping child.

Staring up at the heavens with a pair of glassy, sightless eyes...

Kailas dropped the shovel and went scrambling out of the grave. Dylan looked like he wanted to follow, but stayed out of unshakable loyalty to his friend. His face paled as he took a step closer, reaching out to Cassiel with a trembling hand.

"Cass," he murmured, at a loss for words, "maybe it isn't what you think. The witches might have placed a curse—"

"No." Cassiel was quiet, but he was sure. He lay the dwarf gently back in the earth before climbing out of the grave, shivering slightly in the open air. "I've seen something like this before."

"When?" Katerina asked breathlessly.

"Almost five hundred years ago." His dark eyes stared off into the distance, seeing things the others could not. "When I was growing up."

Chapter 15

They reburied the dwarf. Wrapped him tightly back in his shroud and lay him in the earth. It was done quietly. Respectfully. When they were finished, Tanya lay a sprig of flowers on the grave.

No one asked Cassiel a single question. Even if Dylan wasn't standing in front of him like a guard dog waiting to attack, they doubted they would have gotten much of a response. The fae had tuned out the second he saw the dwarf's blind eyes. His sister was the same way.

It wasn't until they started walking back through the woods, the tall grass folding under their feet, that the fae found his voice—launching unprompted into the story, speaking in a quiet rush.

"When I was sixteen, five children went hiking in the forest near my home. It wasn't uncommon, nor was it unsafe. The world then wasn't like what it is now. People could travel unmolested from realm to realm. Children could play outside without fear of harm."

There was a sudden hitch in his voice. He pulled in a faltering breath.

"No one even thought to look for them. It was two days before we found the bodies."

The gang wasn't moving anymore. They were clustered in a tight group. Staring at him with wide eyes. An evening breeze picked up around them, making everyone shiver.

"I was only a child myself," Cassiel murmured. "I didn't understand what the people around me were saying. Why there was such panic in their eyes, such fear. It wasn't until a few days later that I began to see it for myself. That I began to feel the change."

He trailed off, overcome with emotion, and his sister went to take his hand. Katerina turned to Dylan in confusion, desperate to understand.

"What is he talking about?" she whispered. "What change?"

Dylan stared at the siblings, quietly holding each other as the sky above them darkened to reveal a blanket of stars. After a drawn-out moment, his head bowed with a sigh. "The way my mother explained it, all magic comes from somewhere. Wizards created spells and enchantments. Fairies get their power from the sun—their magic is pure light. The Fae are different. All that they are comes from the heavens. The moon, the stars—all the celestial hosts. But they don't horde it the way some creatures do. They channel that energy back to earth. Keep things in perfect balance. It's one of the ways the sorcerers were able to defeat them in the Great War. Not just by attacking their armies, but by attacking their land."

Katerina shook her head, silently cursing the tutor she'd had growing up at the castle. The man who'd taught her a very selective, imperious version of events.

"What does that mean?" she pressed quietly, casting anxious glances at the fae. "Setting forest fires, poisoning the rivers, ritualistic sacrifice of doves?"

Dylan shook his head, looking abruptly sad. "They polluted the light. Introduced dark magic. Disrupted the natural harmony that the Fae need to survive. Those kids in the woods, the dwarf... it's just a taste of the way things were."

A sudden chill swept up the back of Katerina's legs, making her shiver.

"Or the way things will be again," Aidan muttered. She hadn't heard him approach but he was suddenly standing right beside her, looking as jittery as she had ever seen. "Dylan, we should go back. The dwarf, the wind... I don't like it. We should get inside."

The wind? Is there wind?

Katerina glanced up in surprise just as an icy gale swept her hair into a fiery cloud. It had come out of nowhere, bearing down on the peaceful woods. Far too cold to be seasonable. Far too sudden to make sense. But it wasn't just the wind that worried her. It was something else.

What the heck is happening?

An abstract caution was hovering on the periphery of her mind. An instinctual warning she couldn't make sense of. Like someone was screaming to get her attention, but she was standing too far away to hear. It crept up slowly, prickling the skin on the back of her neck.

"Dylan!" Aidan said again, more urgently this time. "We should leave. *Now.*"

The ranger nodded, but his feet stayed rooted to the ground. He was staring into the trees with a slightly bewildered expression, like he was hearing things that weren't really there. A baby crying. People shouting back and forth. The scream of horses. His mother's voice.

Katerina didn't know why she seemed to know his thoughts, but for some reason it felt like she knew what he was thinking.

Dylan's face whitened and he took a faltering step towards the trees. "Mom...?"

What?!

One step, then another. Aidan lifted a hand to stop him, but before he could a tiny dagger spun through the air—grazing the side of his pale face.

"Leave him alone!"

Katerina whirled around in shock to see Tanya racing towards them. Her bright eyes were fixed on the vampire, and even as she ran she pulled another blade from her belt.

"Tan, what are you doing?!" Katerina cried.

Aidan merely stared in shock, lifting a hand to touch the blood on his cheek.

"Get away from him, Kat!" the shape-shifter screeched. "He's going to kill you!"

Time seemed to slow down as the knife sailed from her fingers, whipping through the air with deadly precision and speed. Katerina saw only the glint of silver as it sailed past her, but Aidan had no intention of getting hit twice. Instead of ducking out of the way he caught the blade between his fingers, stared at it for a moment, then stormed towards Tanya with fangs bared.

...with FANGS bared?!

"Aidan—don't!" Katerina screamed.

The wind carried off her words, then echoed them back a hundred times over. Twisted and cruel. Shrieking with high-pitched laughter. Flying back louder and louder every time.

She dropped into a crouch, covering her head while sucking in broken gasps of air. It was too loud to move. Too loud to think. A second later, she realized her ears had begun to bleed.

"Dylan!" she cried. The wind started mocking that, too, contorting it in strange and frightening ways. "Dylan—help me!"

The ranger tilted his head towards her, but his eyes never left the trees. Those faceless whispers were drawing him closer, further and further away from the group.

"I'm sorry, love," he called distractedly over his shoulder. "Did you say something?"

The fae were frozen, in a world all to themselves. Aidan and Tanya were set on a collision course that was sure to leave one of them bleeding, and the other dead. And Kailas? Katerina lifted her head just high enough to scan the forest floor. Kailas was nowhere to be found.

"DYLAN!" she screeched again. It came back at her a thousand times, shattering her ears, blinding her eyes, splintering her very bones. "SNAP OUT OF IT!"

Still nothing.

She pressed her face into the ground as he walked calmly away from her, completely oblivious to what was happening just behind his back. The edges of the world began to dim and she clawed at the dirt, pulling in just enough air to shout one final thing.

"YOUR MOM'S DEAD!"

It was like she'd doused him in cold water. One second he was walking into the trees with a beatific smile, the next, he was jerking back—blinking quickly, as if he'd been pulled out of a dream.

That's when he heard the screaming. And saw the chaos behind him.

"Shit!" he cried, racing back towards them.

When you live out on your own long enough, you learn to triage. The problems were dealt with in the order of priority, with some skilled multi-tasking along the way.

Dylan sprinted across the forest floor, tackling Aidan just a second before he could snap Tanya's slender neck. The two of them tumbled into the dirt, but the force of the blow seemed to have shaken the vampire out of his murderous trance. He froze in shock, dark hair spilling over the fallen leaves, but Dylan was already racing away, shouting a single command over his shoulder.

"Find Kailas!"

The fae were ignored, as they didn't seem to be in any immediate danger. Without the target of her homicidal rage Tanya had begun weaving together chains of wildflowers, singing under her breath. The vampire was looking for the prince, which just left one more person. The girl cringing against the ground like her skull was about to explode.

"Sweetheart, I'm here!" Dylan slid to his knees beside her. "What can I do? What's wrong?"

What's wrong?! Can't he hear?!

"The screaming," Katerina whispered, sinking further into the ground. "I can't...I can't take it anymore." She lifted her bloody hands to show him, whimpering in pain. "It's breaking my ears."

"...screaming?" Dylan glanced quickly at her palms, before paling in fear. "Honey, there's nothing on your hands. I can't fix this if—"

She screamed again, falling forward onto the grass. The noise seemed to fill every inch of her body. Stretching, expanding, tearing her to pieces as it tried to get out.

"Kat!"

Dylan caught her before she could hit the ground, then held her tightly to his chest. His eyes roved wildly over the clearing, but found nothing to help him. Only the gentle splash of the stream.

"Please let this work..."

With a silent prayer, he swept her into his arms and ran full-tilt towards the water. It wasn't deep this close to the castle, but he didn't need much. Sprays of sand flew into the air as he tore across the shoreline and leapt into the sparkling waves, taking his girlfriend right along with him.

Katerina let out a shout as they plunged into the icy stream, but a torrent of water filled her mouth and the noise was lost beneath the waves. Instead, she fought instinctively against the arm holding her—clawing the skin as she kicked desperately to the surface.

Her head broke through a second later. Only to see Dylan right by her side.

"Did it work?" he asked frantically. "The screaming—is it gone?"

She stared back at him in a daze, unable to process what had happened.

"...the screaming?"

His hands came up to her face, holding it steady so he could look into her eyes.

"Honey, talk to me. I could never hear it, but you... is it gone?"

Her mind raced as she tried to piece it all together. Tried to make sense of the fragments and snapshots she had seen. She remembered now falling to the ground; she remembered going into the water. But something was missing. Something she couldn't quite—

"*Cassiel*," she gasped.

Dylan stared at her for a moment before he forced his face into a smile.

"It's actually Dylan, remember?"

Her hands clamped down on his as her face paled in horror.

"Cass... his eyes..."

It was only then that she remembered. The thing no one else had noticed in the fray. The tiny detail she'd spotted before collapsing in a pile on the ground.

There wasn't a speck of color in the fae's lovely eyes.

Dylan didn't need to wait for an explanation. He didn't need anything besides those three words. The second they left her mouth, he was on his feet and running again. Running as if the world itself had caught fire. Running like a part of him was terrified to stop.

"CASS!"

He reached the clearing at the same time that Aidan and Kailas were coming back. The queen was just a few seconds behind. The vampire gestured to the prince before collapsing on a nearby rock, looking as exhausted as Katerina had ever seen.

"As requested, one Damaris prince. He was—" He cut off suddenly, flashing a quick glance at Kailas' stricken face. "Doesn't matter. Point is that he's back."

Dylan barely heard him. His every thought was centered on one thing.

"CASSIEL!" he shouted again, racing towards the fae.

Now that she was closer, it was easy to see a strange intention to the way the siblings had frozen. Serafina was angled halfway behind her brother, with his strong arm wrapped around her waist. From the way she was tilting off balance it was clear that he'd pulled her suddenly behind his body, protecting her from whatever was to come.

Katerina let out a broken sob as she remembered how the fae had shielded her the same way when they were pounding on the door of the Talsing Sanctuary—a thousand arrows flying at their back. He'd pulled her out of the line of fire, using his own body as a shield.

Perhaps that was the reason Serafina's eyes were still a sparkling onyx, while his were—

"Cass—wake up!"

Dylan shook him roughly, just as Kailas raced forward to attend to his sister. She let out a weak gasp, then collapsed in the prince's arms. Battered, but not broken.

Her brother was a different story.

"Cass—"

Without a word of warning, the fae dropped to his knees. Only the ranger's quick hands kept him from falling entirely. His eyes stared blankly at the canopy of trees, blinded by that glassy sheen as the lines of pain slowly vanished from his face. A moment after that... he stopped breathing.

A wave of shock ripped through Katerina's body. She dropped to her knees.

"...Dylan?"

One look at his face confirmed it. She had never seen a face like that before.

No!

There was a loud ringing in the queen's ears, loud enough to drown out everything else happening in the little clearing. She watched in what felt like slow motion as Dylan struck his friend in the chest again and again, trying desperately to restart his heart. She saw his lips moving, but heard no sound as he shouted and cursed at the sky. Kailas was holding Serafina's body tightly to his chest, staring at the body of her brother. Aidan lifted a hand to his mouth, freezing suddenly in place.

Only one thing broke through her dark reverie, and it was something that had no place there. A child's lullaby, sung in a quiet, lilting voice.

She lifted her eyes in horror to where Tanya was still sitting obliviously on the edge of the grass, stringing flowers together as the singsong rhyme drifted happily from her lips. She was no longer in any physical danger. No one had even thought—

"Tanya," she tried to speak, but her mouth was dry. That nursery rhyme kept echoing in her head, growing more and more dreadful with every line. "Tanya, wake—" She twisted suddenly from one person to another, propelled by a manic surge of hope. "Aidan, give him your blood!"

What the hell have we been waiting for?! A vampire's blood can heal almost anything!

"Aidan!" she cried again. "Dylan, carry him over!"

Dylan didn't even hear her, he was so lost in a waking nightmare, but the vampire crossed the clearing and lifted her silently to her feet, holding her steady with his arm.

"I can't," he said quietly.

She wrenched herself away from him, glaring up through the tears.

"You HAVE to! Now is no time to—"

"I *can't*," he said again. "A vampire can't share blood with a fae." His eyes tightened as they swept over the fallen prince. "Besides, he's already..."

He trailed off as Dylan let out a wretched cry. Burying his face in his friend's tunic. Grabbing fistfuls of white hair as tears spilled freely down his face.

"Cass, *please!*" he wept uncontrollably, holding on with both hands as he shook the lifeless fae. "*Please* don't do this! Just come back—"

A wave of despair ripped through him, taking his breath.

"Cio," he whispered, pressing his forehead to the fae's chest, "*please* don't go."

The wind died down. The clearing went quiet. A sudden hush fell over the forest, and for a never-ending moment all was still.

Then—

"Wait..." Dylan lifted his head, red-rimmed eyes widening in shock as he placed a tentative hand on Cassiel's chest. "I thought I just..." His eyes shot to Aidan, not trusting himself, unable to believe it might be true. "Did you just—"

"I heard it." Aidan knelt quickly at his side, placing two fingers on the inside of Cassiel's wrist. "I heard a pulse."

They froze perfectly still, listening with intense focus, before their heads snapped up at the same time. Dylan was beside himself with happiness. Aidan was a bit more practical in his relief.

"You need to snap him out of it," he ordered, taking a step back. "I don't know what this is, but we all needed to break free. Shouting, tackling, jumping into cold water... do *something*."

Without pausing a second, Dylan swung his fist right into Cassiel's face. There was a soft cracking sound, followed by a trickle of blood, but otherwise the fae stayed fast asleep.

Katerina and Aidan glanced at each other. Torn between amusement and extreme fear.

"Honey," she inserted delicately, "try something that doesn't break his face."

Dylan nodded quickly, as if the thought had never occurred to him.

Propping up the fae as best he could, he went through a multitude of options. He tried shouting, slapping, dropping, clapping. He even raced back to the river and splashed some freezing cold water in his face. Nothing. And his eyes were just as white as ever.

Katerina watched breathlessly from behind her fingers, offering a silent prayer as that pulse began to fade and they started losing him again. Whatever was going to happen, had to happen now.

"Dylan... hurry."

The ranger stopped what he was doing, giving it a split second's thought before his body went very still. Then, keeping his eyes on the fae the entire time, he started taking off his clothes.

Katerina and Aidan exchanged another look. Slightly more panicked than the last.

"Honey," she interjected once more, "I don't know what you're thinking, but that's not—"

A chocolate brown wolf sprang up in his place.

Oh. Right.

There was a great deal of trepidation as the wolf approached the sleeping fae. Even more so when he nudged him gently with his head. He let out a little sigh, understandable even to human ears. Then, with a look Katerina knew she would never forget, he leapt forward and attacked.

"Holy crap..." She melted backwards, leaning heavily into Aidan's chest. "Isn't there... I mean, there has to be some other way."

He shook his head, staring at the wolf with both respect and fear.

"Whatever this was, Cass got it a lot worse than the rest of us. We all lost our grip on reality, but he...he was about two seconds away from ending up like that dwarf we just buried."

They both flinched as the beast tore into him again and again.

"Yeah, but *that*?" Katerina asked silently.

Aidan winced sympathetically, tightening his grip on her shoulder.

"We want him to wake up... and that *has* to hurt."

It wasn't easy for a shifter to censor himself to begin with, and Dylan did absolutely nothing to check himself now. Short of going for the jugular, everything else was on the table. And while it might have been killing him to do so, he took his time—inflicting the maximum amount of pain.

For a while, nothing seemed to be happening. No matter how many times the wolf came at him, Cassiel lay perfectly still upon the ground.

Bleeding quietly.

Lost to the world.

Lost to them.

Until, all of a sudden—he moved.

"*Yes*," Katerina whispered, cupping her hands over her mouth.

With a bark of excitement, the wolf sank his teeth into the fae's leg—thrashing him back and forth.

Cassiel let out a quiet gasp then slowly opened his eyes, blinking blindly as he tried to pull himself free. The wolf bit down even harder, prompting a soft cry.

"His eyes—" Katerina tried to race forward, but Aidan caught her by the hand.

"Just give it time."

It was one of the most terrible things Katerina had ever seen, while being impossibly sweet at the same time. Every bit of hurt Dylan inflicted, he internalized tenfold. Every time the fae cried out in fear or pain, a little part of him withered away. At one point, when Cassiel actually called to Dylan for help, she thought her boyfriend might never recover.

But, heartbreaking as it was, his plan was working.

The pain focused Cassiel's mind, sharpened his senses, fought back whatever dark power had him under its spell. A few minutes after he woke up, that terrifying whiteness began to clear from his sparkling eyes. A few minutes after that, he came to enough to realize where he was.

"...D-Dylan?"

The wolf vanished immediately and the ranger appeared in his place. Throwing a cloak hurriedly over his shoulders, he dove to the ground by Cassiel's side, propping him up as gently as possible while Aidan and Katerina rushed to his other side.

"Are you all right?" Dylan asked breathlessly. "Can you...can you see?"

A fist swung out of nowhere, promptly shattering his nose.

"*Really?*" Cassiel lifted his head with a weak smile. "You couldn't think of *any* other way?"

For the first time in Dylan's life, a sarcastic comeback failed him. The witty repartee fell short on his tongue. He simply let out a breathless gasp and grabbed the fae in his arms. Forgetting any sense of pride or shame as he held him in a tight embrace. Cassiel froze a moment in surprise, then embraced him back—looking abruptly protective, though he was the one still bleeding.

"It's been a long time since you called me that," he murmured, pulling back with a gentle smile. "...Cio."

Dylan flushed and looked at the ground, while Katerina slipped her hand into his.

"What does it mean?" she whispered.

Cassiel gave her hand a squeeze, never taking his eyes off the ranger. "It means brother."

A thoughtful silence fell over the group as each one took a quiet moment to think about what had been saved, what had almost been lost. Then a carefree voice shattered the stillness and Cassiel looked over their heads to where his girlfriend was still singing happily amongst the flowers.

"She took it well, didn't she?"

Katerina pushed quickly to her feet, rushing over with a hasty apology. "I'm so sorry, she didn't even know. Just keep resting, Cass, this will just take a minute."

But Cassiel didn't want to take a minute. In fact, they didn't have a minute to spare.

Ignoring the warnings of everyone around him he pushed lightly to his feet, holding out his arm as his girlfriend stopped dancing and slowing turned around. She seemed to crash back to reality and raced automatically to his side.

"What the hell just happened?" she asked in a daze. "Kat said you'd been hurt..."

The others shared a dark look, but said nothing.

"I'll be fine," Cassiel kissed her swiftly before gesturing to the castle, "but we have to get back to the castle. *Now*. I'm afraid we don't have a lot of time."

Chapter 16

"It is *exactly* the same," Cassiel said as the lot of them hurried back through the trees. His sister was still only half-conscious in Kailas' arms, but the rest of them were keeping pace. "*Exactly* the same as it was before. At the very start of things. The beginning of the war."

"But how can that be?" Tanya asked reasonably. "You told me that...that *darkness* was the creation of wizards. Carpathian mercenaries, creatures of the Dunes. The war started for a reason, Cass. There was a man behind it, calling the shots. Who could be doing it now?"

"I don't know," he said softly, eyes on the drawbridge, "but I intend to find out."

The entire way back from the forest it had been the same looping argument. No one had any idea how such terrible forces could have been resurrected without anyone in the five kingdoms being the wiser, and yet there was no other explanation for what had happened in the woods.

Cassiel was on one side, Tanya was on the other, while Katerina and Aidan were on the fence. Dylan was too happy his friend had come back from the dead to dare disagree with him, Serafina was unconscious, and Kailas kept swearing up and down that this 'darkness' wasn't him.

All they knew for certain was that some evil force had clearly descended upon the High Kingdom and that the rest of the castle must immediately be warned. Maybe the rest of them would know what to do. Maybe the councils would have some information the others did not.

"I know you hate it when I say this, Tanya, but you're very young." Cassiel swept quickly over the drawbridge, the others following close by his side. "You haven't seen the kinds of things I have, haven't lived through them. I *know* what happened in the forest. I've felt it before."

"I'm just saying, we need to consider this from all angles," she countered. "For all we know, this is some rogue wizard acting on his own just like Alwyn. What we need is a little more time—"

But, as fate would have it, *time* was not going to be a factor.

The castle doors swung open and the seven friends stopped where they stood. Mouths falling open. Eyes widening in shock. Falling perfectly silent as the door behind them banged shut.

They're all... frozen.

It was a castle full of statues. As if someone had simply stopped the hands of time.

Like Sleeping Beauty.

A Belarian nobleman was paused as he walked down the stairs, one foot hovering above the floor. A pair of servants was frozen in a deep bow while another was suspended in front of a portrait, her feather duster still reaching into the air. Guards were paused mid-conversation; a Kreo pixie was frozen with a cup of nectar half-lifted to her mouth.

Katerina jumped back with a start to see Hastings, her beloved protector, standing perfectly still by the door, a belated twinkle still dancing in his eyes.

No one looked frightened. No one looked as if they were in pain.

They were all just... stuck.

"What happened here?" Serafina asked with a gasp, waking suddenly for the first time. Her boyfriend set her down as the others gawked at the frozen castle.

Dylan stepped forward, looking uncharacteristically grave. "I don't know..."

A sudden crash from the ceiling made them all duck and then lift their heads.

"...but we're not alone."

THE END

Protected Blurb:

The Queen's Alpha Series

Eternal
Everlasting
Unceasing
Evermore
Forever
Boundless
Prophecy
Protected
Foretelling
Revelation
Betrayal
Resolved

Find W.J. May

Website:
http://www.wanitamay.yolasite.com
Facebook:
https://www.facebook.com/pages/Author-WJ-May-FAN-PAGE/
141170442608149
Newsletter:
SIGN UP FOR W.J. May's Newsletter to find out about new releases,
updates, cover reveals and even freebies!
http://eepurl.com/97aYf

More books by W.J. May

The Chronicles of Kerrigan

BOOK I - *Rae of Hope* **is FREE!**
Book Trailer:
http://www.youtube.com/watch?v=gILAwXxx8MU
Book II - *Dark Nebula*
Book Trailer:
http://www.youtube.com/watch?v=Ca24STi_bFM
Book III - *House of Cards*
Book IV - *Royal Tea*
Book V - *Under Fire*
Book VI - *End in Sight*
Book VII – *Hidden Darkness*
Book VIII – *Twisted Together*
Book IX – *Mark of Fate*
Book X – *Strength & Power*
Book XI – *Last One Standing*
BOOK XII – *Rae of Light*

PREQUEL –
Christmas Before the Magic
Question the Darkness
Into the Darkness
Fight the Darkness
Alone the Darkness
Lost the Darkness

SEQUEL –
Matter of Time
Time Piece
Second Chance
Glitch in Time
Our Time
Precious Time

Hidden Secrets Saga:
Download Seventh Mark part 1 For FREE
Book Trailer:
http://www.youtube.com/watch?v=Y-_vVYC1gvo

Like most teenagers, Rouge is trying to figure out who she is and what she wants to be. With little knowledge about her past, she has questions but has never tried to find the answers. Everything changes when she befriends a strangely intoxicating family. Siblings Grace and Michael, appear to have secrets which seem connected to Rouge. Her hunch is confirmed when a horrible incident occurs at an outdoor party. Rouge may be the only one who can find the answer.

An ancient journal, a Sioghra necklace and a special mark force life-altering decisions for a girl who grew up unprepared to fight for her life or others.

All secrets have a cost and Rouge's determination to find the truth can only lead to trouble...or something even more sinister.

RADIUM HALOS - THE SENSELESS SERIES
Book 1 is FREE

Everyone needs to be a hero at one point in their life.

The small town of Elliot Lake will never be the same again.

Caught in a sudden thunderstorm, Zoe, a high school senior from Elliot Lake, and five of her friends take shelter in an abandoned uranium mine. Over the next few days, Zoe's hearing sharpens drastically, beyond what any normal human being can detect. She tells her friends, only to learn that four others have an increased sense as well. Only Kieran, the new boy from Scotland, isn't affected.

Fashioning themselves into superheroes, the group tries to stop the strange occurrences happening in their little town. Muggings, break-ins, disappearances, and murder begin to hit too close to home. It leads the team to think someone knows about their secret - someone who wants them all dead.

An incredulous group of heroes. A traitor in the midst. Some dreams are written in blood.

Courage Runs Red
The Blood Red Series
Book 1 is FREE

WHAT IF COURAGE WAS your only option?

When Kallie lands a college interview with the city's new hot-shot police officer, she has no idea everything in her life is about to change. The detective is young, handsome and seems to have an unnatural ability to stop the increasing local crime rate. Detective Liam's particular interest in Kallie sends her heart and head stumbling over each other.

When a raging blood feud between vampires spills into her home, Kallie gets caught in the middle. Torn between love and family loyalty she must find the courage to fight what she fears the most and possibly risk everything, even if it means dying for those she loves.

Daughter of Darkness - Victoria
Only Death Could Stop Her Now
The Daughters of Darkness is a series of female heroines who may or
may not know each other, but all have the same father, Vlad Montour.
Victoria is a Hunter Vampire

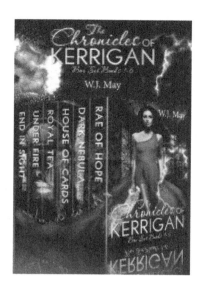

Did you love *Prophecy*? Then you should read *Courage Runs Red* by W.J. May!

What if courage was your only option?

When Kallie lands a college interview with the city's new hot-shot police officer, she has no idea everything in her life is about to change. The detective is young, handsome and seems to have an unnatural ability to stop the increasing local crime rate. Detective Liam's particular interest in Kallie sends her heart and head stumbling over each other.

When a raging blood feud between vampires spills into her home, Kallie gets caught in the middle. Torn between love and family loyalty she must find the courage to fight what she fears the most and possibly risk everything, even if it means dying for those she loves.

Fall in love with immortar vampires and werewolves in this paranormal fantasy series.

Blood Red Series:

Courage Runs Red
Night Watch
Marked by Courage
Forever Night

Read more at https://www.facebook.com/USA-TODAY-Best-seller-WJ-May-Author-141170442608149/.

Also by W.J. May

Bit-Lit Series
Lost Vampire
Cost of Blood
Price of Death

Blood Red Series
Courage Runs Red
The Night Watch
Marked by Courage
Forever Night

Daughters of Darkness: Victoria's Journey
Victoria
Huntress
Coveted (A Vampire & Paranormal Romance)
Twisted
Daughter of Darkness - Victoria - Box Set

Hidden Secrets Saga
Seventh Mark - Part 1
Seventh Mark - Part 2
Marked By Destiny
Compelled
Fate's Intervention
Chosen Three
The Hidden Secrets Saga: The Complete Series

Kerrigan Chronicles
Stopping Time
A Passage of Time
Ticking Clock

Mending Magic Series
Lost Souls
Illusion of Power

Paranormal Huntress Series
Never Look Back
Coven Master
Alpha's Permission
Blood Bonding
Oracle of Nightmares
Shadows in the Night
Paranormal Huntress BOX SET #1-3

Prophecy Series
Only the Beginning
White Winter
Secrets of Destiny

The Chronicles of Kerrigan
Rae of Hope
Dark Nebula
House of Cards
Royal Tea
Under Fire
End in Sight
Hidden Darkness
Twisted Together
Mark of Fate
Strength & Power
Last One Standing
Rae of Light
The Chronicles of Kerrigan Box Set Books # 1 - 6

The Chronicles of Kerrigan: Gabriel
Living in the Past
Present For Today
Staring at the Future

The Chronicles of Kerrigan Prequel

Christmas Before the Magic
Question the Darkness
Into the Darkness
Fight the Darkness
Alone in the Darkness
Lost in Darkness
The Chronicles of Kerrigan Prequel Series Books #1-3

The Chronicles of Kerrigan Sequel
A Matter of Time
Time Piece
Second Chance
Glitch in Time
Our Time
Precious Time

The Hidden Secrets Saga
Seventh Mark (part 1 & 2)

The Queen's Alpha Series
Eternal
Everlasting
Unceasing
Evermore
Forever
Boundless
Prophecy
Protected

Foretelling

The Senseless Series
Radium Halos
Radium Halos - Part 2
Nonsense

Standalone
Shadow of Doubt (Part 1 & 2)
Five Shades of Fantasy
Shadow of Doubt - Part 1
Shadow of Doubt - Part 2
Four and a Half Shades of Fantasy
Dream Fighter
What Creeps in the Night
Forest of the Forbidden
Arcane Forest: A Fantasy Anthology
The First Fantasy Box Set

Watch for more at https://www.facebook.com/USA-TODAY-Best-seller-WJ-May-Author-141170442608149/.

About the Author

About W.J. May

Welcome to USA TODAY BESTSELLING author W.J. May's Page! SIGN UP for W.J. May's Newsletter to find out about new releases, updates, cover reveals and even freebies! http://eepurl.com/97aYf http://www.facebook.com/pages/Author-WJ-May-FAN-PAGE/ 141170442608149?ref=hl and http://www.wanitamay.yolasite.com/ *Please feel free to connect with me and share your comments. I love connecting with my readers.* W.J. May grew up in the fruit belt of Ontario. Crazy-happy childhood, she always has had a vivid imagination and loads of energy. After her father passed away in 2008, from a six-year battle with cancer (which she still believes he won the fight against), she began to write again. A passion she'd loved for years, but realized life was too short to keep putting it off. She is a writer of Young Adult, Fantasy Fiction and where ever else her little muses take her.

Read more at https://www.facebook.com/USA-TODAY-Best-seller-WJ-May-Author-141170442608149/.

Made in the USA
Monee, IL
27 January 2021

58882338R00118